# The Barefoot Wedding

## MARRIED IN MALIBU

## BOOK 3

# LUCY KEVIN

**THE BAREFOOT WEDDING**

Married in Malibu, Book 3

© 2018 Lucy Kevin

**Sign up for Lucy's Newsletter**

lucykevin.com/newsletter

**www.LucyKevin.com**

As the head of security for Married in Malibu, Travis Houston is absolutely certain that no one will ever get into one of their celebrity beachfront weddings without an invitation, particularly the paparazzi. But though he's a master at keeping his clients safe, he can't say the same for keeping his own heart safe. Especially when Amy Woodford shows up from out of the blue and completely takes his breath away.

Three years ago, Amy went halfway across the country to try to escape heartbreak. But when her best friend's wedding brings her to Married in Malibu, she's suddenly face-to-face with the man she once loved with all her heart.

Love is always in the air at the beach in Malibu, and this summer is no exception as Travis and Amy can't help but fall for each other all over again. But will Amy's unconditional love be enough for Travis to believe that he can be good enough to transcend the pain from his past and give her his entire heart?

# Chapter One

The heavy rain caught Amy Woodford by surprise, and that alone reminded her just how long she'd been away from Southern California. Locals knew that while it rarely rained in Malibu, when it did, it *poured*.

She hadn't yet come to feel like a native of her adopted Michigan, but somewhere in the last three years, she'd forgotten enough about California to start buying into the myth that there were only ever cloudless blue skies. Even on the plane when she'd seen the storm clouds gathering, Amy had been certain that the sun would be shining once she landed. And for another hour, the rain had held off. Long enough for her to drop her bag off at the beachfront rental house as the sun set, then change into a pretty dress and redo her makeup before heading to Married in Malibu, the boutique wedding venue for the stars.

Maya Lamsen, Amy's best friend, was going to marry Nolan Ruccolo, the love of her life, next weekend. As Maya's maid of honor, Amy was here several days ahead of the wedding to take care of the last-minute details, while her supermodel friend wrapped up a high-budget photo shoot.

Amy was determined to make sure that Maya and Nolan had the perfect wedding. So determined, in fact, that she was willingly heading back into a very dangerous emotional place...with the only man who had ever captured, then crushed, her heart.

"Everything is going to be fine," she promised herself as she parked her rental car at the wedding venue.

It had to be.

There was nothing that could have possibly kept Amy from being there for Maya on the most special day of her friend's life. Not the rain that had finally started to pour down from the dark clouds above, turning from droplets to a vertical river in a matter of seconds.

And definitely not *him*.

Fighting the urge to get back into her car and drive away, Amy ran toward the front door through the quickly forming puddles in the parking lot. Taking off her heels so that she could move quicker, she did her best to ignore the scrape of the pavement against her feet. But it was just as impossible to outrun the rain as it was to pretend the small pebbles in the parking lot didn't hurt.

Some things you just can't run away from.

And you can't pretend they aren't happening either.

Her clothes were soaked through by the time she got to the door and rang the bell. So much for making a good impression. The storm had tangled her hair into a wild and unruly mess, her dress was plastered to her, her feet were muddy, and she didn't even want to think about the state of her makeup.

Had it been a sunny day, the wedding venue would likely have been the most beautiful spot imaginable, with the converted hotel forming a centerpiece in the blooming gardens and a path leading down to a small, private beach. But she was too wet, and too nervous, to appreciate any of that today.

When there was no answer to the bell, Amy thumped her fist against the door, desperate to get out of the rain, then looked up at the small dome of a security camera above the door. "Could someone please let me in? I'm here to help with my friend's wedding."

At last, Amy was relieved to hear footsteps and then the click and snap of someone unlocking the door. But her relief was short-lived.

Because Travis Houston was standing barely a foot away.

Built like a star football player, he wore a tailored suit that emphasized his strength and power, as did his military-short hair. His caramel skin made his dark eyes stand out as they looked her over. She knew that he would take in every last detail, because he always had.

Somehow, she found her voice. "Hello, Travis."

★ ★ ★

*Amy Woodford.*

Though Travis had seen her on the security camera, he still couldn't believe the most beautiful woman he'd ever known was standing on the doorstep of Married in Malibu.

"Can I come in?" Amy asked, and it was only then that Travis realized he was staring at her while she continued to be drenched by the rain blowing in from the parking lot.

He hurriedly stepped back. "Of course. Come in. Let me find you a towel to dry off with, and maybe a blanket too."

During his career, he'd faced down paparazzi and crowds that had threatened to get out of control, without so much as blinking. Yet, Amy's presence had him reeling.

Travis gave her a towel from the linen cupboards and then a blanket that she wrapped around herself in an effort to get warm, before bringing her to his office. He made them both tea, partly because it was a good way to get some heat back into her...and partly because he needed something to do with his hands so that he didn't give in to the urge to pull her into his arms. She was still shivering slightly as she gratefully cupped the mug of peppermint tea in her hands and took a sip.

"What are you doing here?" he asked, his surprise at seeing her again making his voice gruffer than usual.

"I'm the maid of honor for my friend Maya's wedding this weekend," Amy replied. "She couldn't get away from work, so I flew in from Michigan to check on the last-minute details for her."

Travis silently digested the information. He hadn't let himself look for Amy after she left Los Angeles, because if he had, it would have been way too tempting to jump on a plane to go after her. And to beg her to come back to him.

"I wasn't expecting you to show up like this," Travis admitted.

"I can see that," Amy replied, her expression unreadable.

"What I meant," he clarified, "is that I don't remember seeing your name on the guest list."

"I used the name Amy Willington for Maya's guest list," she said in a soft voice.

"You're married?" The thought that she had fallen in love with someone else was a lead weight in Travis's chest.

"No, I'm not married."

The relief that washed through him was as powerful as the waves that washed in against the beach.

"I knew you worked here," she continued, "and I

didn't want to cause any problems for anyone, so I used my mother's maiden name."

"Seeing you again isn't a problem," he assured her. Yes, his heart felt like it was rocketing around inside his chest, but at least he felt *something* again. As opposed to the numbness of the past three years. "How have you been doing?"

"I got an opportunity to paint in Michigan after..." She let her words fall away, obviously not wanting to talk about what had happened between them. "So I took it."

Travis knew Amy had attended art school in spite of her parents' wishes—and their disapproval of her chosen career. He had always been proud of her for going after her dreams. "That's great that your painting is going so well. I always knew that it would."

Emotion flashed in her eyes before the shutters fell again. "Actually, I haven't made all that many sales yet."

That wasn't what Travis had expected to hear. Amy was so talented and determined. If anyone deserved success with her art, she did. He wanted to ask what had happened and why it wasn't working out quite the way she'd hoped. But he couldn't. The same way that he couldn't reach out to put his arms around her. Because he didn't have the right to do it anymore.

His old feelings might be bubbling away under the surface, drawing him to her, but the simple fact was that he wasn't worthy of her.

He never had been.

Besides, it was obvious that Amy wasn't comfortable talking about her painting career. Even with the blanket wrapped around her, she looked less at ease now than she had standing on the doorstep, soaked to the bone by the rain.

"Maya asked me to take a look at the wedding and reception plans. I know it's after hours for the rest of the staff here, but if there is any chance you could show them to me, I'd really appreciate it."

Though he knew it made sense for them to get back on a purely business track, it was still extremely difficult to mask his disappointment that she was done talking about herself. "Yes, of course."

Amy kept the blanket around her while Travis led the way to Meg's office, where they could look at the detailed drawings for the ceremony and wedding reception, along with the lighting plans. There were also samples of the linens, as well as drawings of the flower selections.

Amy lifted the drawings to the light, looking at them from different angles for several minutes. Finally, she said, "Whoever put this together is a genius. Both the drawings and the design sensibility are absolutely perfect."

"Meg is a brilliant designer," Travis agreed. "Will

you be able to come back tomorrow to meet her and the others to discuss the plans in detail? Everyone should be in by nine o'clock."

"Nine sounds fine." When she looked up into his eyes, he found himself hoping she might be about to say something more—maybe about how she missed him, or that she hoped they could try again. But in the end, she simply said, "Thanks for letting me in and showing me the plans. I probably shouldn't have come by so late, but I couldn't wait until tomorrow morning to take a quick peek at things."

Travis knew he should take her words at face value. Still, he couldn't help but hope the real reason she had come tonight wasn't just because she was helping her friend with her wedding, but because she'd wanted to see *him*.

Now that she was here, standing before him looking as bright and beautiful as ever, he didn't want her to go so soon. Not when it had been so long.

Far too long.

So as he walked her to the door, he couldn't stop himself from saying, "Would you like to go out and get some dinner?"

Amy blinked at him, looking momentarily stunned. And, for a split second, tempted. But then she shook her head. "I ate on the plane. Thanks again for your help tonight. I'll see you tomorrow."

Before he knew it, she had taken off the blanket, bundled it into his hands, and fled to her car. Then she was gone.

# Chapter Two

Travis stayed in the doorway long after Amy's car disappeared from sight. It wasn't until it finally stopped raining that he drew himself away to close up for the night.

Securing the venue was a simple process of setting alarms and checking that doors were properly locked. But when he had to type in the code for the alarms a third time, his fingers nearly fumbling over the numbers yet again, it was impossible to pretend that seeing Amy tonight hadn't deeply impacted him.

For the last three years, he'd done his best to be happy. There were even moments here or there when it felt like he'd succeeded. His job running security at Married in Malibu had done more than anything else to take his mind off the past.

But now that Amy was back?

He couldn't possibly look into her eyes and feel nothing.

Nor could he keep the memories he'd pushed away

about the day he'd begun to fall for her from flooding back.

* * *

*Three years ago…*

The Malibu farmers' market was so crowded with people buying organically grown fruit and vegetables that he almost didn't hear his name being called.

Turning, Travis was surprised to see the beautiful woman from the check-in desk at his gym waving to him. Her name was Amy, and he'd been struck from the first by her sweetness and warmth. Today, she looked as lovely as ever in jeans and a royal blue T-shirt that matched her eyes.

He was just turning to make his way toward her when her shopping bag split, sending apricots and apples and potatoes spilling out and tumbling to the ground. Travis's size was a bonus when he hurried to her side, as the crowd had no choice but to part to let him through.

"Here," he said as he got down on the ground with her to pick up her fruits and vegetables, "let me help."

"This wasn't exactly the impression I was hoping to make," she said, her cheeks flushed as she picked up an apple and put it into her bag.

Travis tilted his head slightly. "You were hoping to make an impression on me?"

"The next time I saw you, I mean. I wasn't…" She paused, flushing even deeper now. "Sorry, I'm making this sound like I'm stalking you or something."

Travis smiled. "I hope I would have noticed if you were, given that keeping people from being stalked is my job."

"True," Amy said, returning his smile.

After they had picked everything up and stowed her bag in the trunk of her car, she surprised him yet again. "Please let me take you for coffee to say thank you."

"I was happy to help." Travis didn't want her to think she owed him for anything. "But I'd still like to join you for coffee."

They found a café halfway down the block, and Travis automatically chose a booth with a view of the door and decent access to the rear exits. As a bodyguard, it was habit.

"This is a great spot," Amy said. "The light coming in through the window is just perfect."

She saw the world in a way that had nothing to do with safety or preparation and everything to do with beauty. Despite the hard-won lessons of his past, Travis was drawn to her bright perspective.

After she ordered a mocha with extra chocolate sprinkles and he decided on an espresso, she pulled a small sketchbook out of her purse. "Would you mind if I drew you?"

No one had ever asked him something like that before. And though he wondered why she would want to draw him, of all people, as soon as he nodded, she plunged into a sketch.

He'd always thought artists were withdrawn, introverted, more focused on things in their head than the people around them. Yet, when Amy drew, it was obvious that she was utterly intent on diving out into the world, to engage with it and explore it.

"Can I see it?" Travis asked.

"Almost. I just need to add in a few little touches."

Nothing about Travis was little, so he couldn't imagine what she was seeing that others didn't. But a few minutes later when she turned the sketch pad around, instead of her sketch portraying him as brooding—or possibly even a little frightening—he was smiling. And looking surprisingly approachable.

Was this really how she saw him?

"I hope you like it," she said, her voice suddenly shy and unsure.

"I do," he said. "It's just that I'm not used to seeing myself looking like this."

"Like what?"

He almost said *happy*. "Smiling and relaxed."

"It's a good look on you."

Was she flirting with him?

And if she was, should he flirt back?

Instead, he said, "Your parents must be really proud of your talent."

Unfortunately, that was when Amy's smile slipped away. "Proud is the wrong word. Embarrassed is more like it."

"Embarrassed?" He didn't hide his confusion. "Why would they be embarrassed when you're so talented?"

"They don't have a lot of time or respect for art." Amy closed her sketchbook, then slipped it back into her bag, her inner light dimmer now. "My family all have serious jobs. 'Real' jobs." She used her hands to make quotation marks around the word. "That you need an MBA or a law degree to do. When I decided to go to art school, they weren't happy."

Travis knew about family problems and how bad they could be. Which was why he had to ask, "What did they do?"

"They cut me off," Amy said, trying to shrug like it didn't matter, though it clearly did. "And then they said that they would be there for me when I finally came around and realized art wasn't going to work as a career." She paused before adding, "My mother thought I was painting just to hurt her."

Travis hated what he was hearing. "You can't hurt anyone by painting."

"I know, but they don't seem to get that it wasn't about them. That I didn't run away to art school because

I didn't want to enter the real world. I went because art is what makes me happy, and I can't imagine doing anything else."

* * *

*Present day...*

Travis shook his head at the memory of Amy looking so sad. Little did she know that he was able to understand, better than probably anyone, what she was going through with her family.

The more he'd gotten to know her over the coming weeks, the harder he'd fallen. She was kind and gentle, sweet and giving, and he would have done absolutely anything to protect her and keep her safe. Surprisingly, she seemed to feel the same way about him.

No one else in his life had ever made him feel that way.

The alarm he was setting chirped, reminding him that he needed to finish signing out for the night. But even as he worked to turn his focus back to his job, he knew it would be impossible to stop thinking of Amy.

And how badly he wished things could have turned out differently.

*Chapter Three*

Amy paused in front of her bedroom mirror the next morning, carefully wiping away some of the blusher from her cheekbones. She'd been determined this morning not to dress up on Travis's account. Yet, here she was in another expensive dress, wearing more makeup than she would wear to the wedding itself.

The problem was that Travis was as tall, dark, and handsome as ever...with eyes that she swore could see all the way into her heart.

Amy could still remember the first time he'd walked into the gym where she'd worked to earn money for rent and food—but mostly art supplies. One conversation with Travis was all it took for her to know that he wasn't like the other guys who came in to lift too-heavy weights and brag about their conquests. Of course he had to work out to stay in shape as a bodyguard, but he was completely discreet and never bragged about any of his clients. Had anyone else in the gym worked as a bodyguard, the place would have echoed with stories of celebrities and fistfights. What's more, Travis always took the time to ask how she was doing. And unlike most guys, he actually listened to her answers.

Seeing Travis at the gym had been the highlight of her days then—she knew she lit up every time he walked through the door. Which was precisely why seeing him again hurt so much. Ever since things had ended between them, a part of her had felt dark and broken.

Maya knew exactly how difficult losing Travis had been for Amy, of course. So though Maya had heard wonderful things about Married in Malibu, and it was clearly the best choice if she wanted to keep the paparazzi from spoiling her wedding, she never would have booked her wedding there if Amy hadn't gone out of her way to reassure her friend that she would be cool and calm and completely unaffected when she saw Travis again.

Today, it was time to make good on that promise.

Leaving the rental house, Amy headed to her car, then set the cardboard tube that held her wedding gift on the passenger seat, strapping it in carefully. She didn't want to risk anything happening to it.

She'd left Maya a message last night to share her first, excellent impressions of Married in Malibu and the wedding plans. Perhaps Amy should have also told her that seeing Travis again had been no big deal. But she hadn't been able to get the lie to come out of her mouth.

As she drove, she reminded herself that she only needed to hold on to her self-control for a few days. And then she would head back to Michigan and Travis would be out of her life again.

Deliberately focusing on the clear blue sky and the sea-salt scent of the ocean rather than her painful memories helped Amy feel more centered by the time she parked in the Married in Malibu lot. And as she pushed the buzzer beside the front door, she was more determined than ever not to lose her cool again.

Travis opened the door a few moments later. "You look beautiful."

Amy had never been what people would call a conventional beauty. Just like with her art, no one but Travis had ever given her the impression that she measured up. The truth was that she had never really felt beautiful until he'd looked at her.

"Thank you," she said, wishing her voice didn't sound so breathless. Unfortunately, she was no better able to stop her reaction to him this morning than she had been last night.

"Did you sleep well?" Travis asked as he stepped aside to let her in.

"I'm still a little jet-lagged," she said, deciding that was better than confessing that she'd tossed and turned all night thinking of him. "I didn't get a chance yesterday to ask how you like working here."

"It's great. Really great."

When silence fell between them, Amy had to stifle a groan. Three years ago, she felt like she could tell him anything, even things she wouldn't have dared say to anybody else. Now, even small talk was difficult. Amy breathed a silent sigh of relief when a smiling woman in a business suit walked up.

"Welcome to Married in Malibu. You must be Maya's friend Amy. I'm Liz Wilkinson, the venue's manager." After they shook hands, Liz said, "I'm so glad you could come a few days early. I'd love to show you everything we have in place for Maya and Nolan's wedding. Why don't we visit the kitchens first?" Liz led the way, with Travis following behind as though guarding them both. "I usually find that once people have tasted one of Jenn's cakes, they'll agree to most things."

"Maya couldn't stop talking about how good Jenn's cakes are," Amy said with an answering smile. "I've been dying to taste them myself."

In the kitchen, a woman was baking, while a man in a photographer's vest munched on a cupcake while scrolling through something on a tablet on the counter in front of him.

"Jenn and Daniel," Liz said, "I'd like you to meet Amy. She's here to look over everything for her friend Maya."

"It's great to meet you, Amy," Jenn said. "The wedding cake is well underway, although we'll be using a stand-in for today's run-through."

Daniel shook her hand next. "I'll be taking photos of the wedding and reception. I'll walk you through my plan, and then if you have any suggestions for changes, we can see about working them in."

Though photography wasn't Amy's specialty, she knew all about Daniel's award-winning work as a photojournalist. If she one day had even a smidgeon of his success with her paintings, she would be happy.

Next, they headed to an office, where a man was sitting behind a bank of monitors. Strangely, he looked more like a lumberjack than a computer expert, with his flannel shirt, faded jeans, and rumpled hair.

"This is Nate," Liz said. "Nate, Amy is here to oversee everything for Maya's wedding."

Nate gave Amy a warm, slightly crooked smile. "I've got the lighting set to run off a laptop, and I'm currently coding in the sequence changes. I'll give a holler once I'm ready to do a live run-through so you can let me know what you think."

Liz led the way back through the building to the main hall. "As you can see, we're nearly done constructing the set for the ceremony and setting out the seats."

Amy took in the rows of seating, the slightly raised stage where Maya and Nolan would say their vows, and the artfully constructed backdrop. Two women were working on it, one in designer slacks and a silk blouse and the other in baggy jeans with her hair bound up beneath a baseball cap.

"Careful, Kate," the put-together woman said. "We don't want to get mud on the drapes."

"And have to answer to you, Meg?" the other woman said with a laugh. "I wouldn't dare."

Travis had sounded so impressed with Meg last night, and Amy could see why. She was glossy, polished, poised.

Everything that Amy wasn't.

And yet, he wasn't exactly falling all over himself to get closer to Meg, was he? Despite herself, Amy was more than a little relieved that his workplace friendship hadn't turned into something more.

After introducing Amy to Meg and Kate, Liz said, "I hope everything looks the way you and Maya expect it to?"

"What I've seen so far looks fantastic," Amy told her.

The design was classic, but with enough color and style that it didn't feel sterile. In the warmth of the Malibu sun, the room practically shone. What's more, everyone on staff was so nice and friendly, especially considering their immense talents. No wonder Travis enjoyed working here so much. Who wouldn't?

"There is one thing I was hoping we could add in, however." Amy's nerves returned with a vengeance as she explained, "I painted a portrait for Maya and Nolan as a surprise, and I would feel much better if I knew it was safe here until the wedding."

"I can't wait to see it," Liz said with a smile.

"Actually, I need to frame it first. I looked online and found a framing store not too far from here. Would it be all right if I brought it back this afternoon?"

"Actually," Liz said, "given Meg's tendency to make sure we have absolutely everything on hand that she could possibly need to outfit the rooms during our weddings, I wouldn't be surprised if we don't already have everything you need to make the frame here. Travis, could you please show Amy where we keep our supplies and give her a hand if need be?"

"It would be my pleasure," he said.

His instant agreement filled Amy with warmth, even though she knew it was what anyone else would have said.

"Perfect." Liz looked expectantly at Amy. "Could you show us the painting now?"

# Chapter Four

Travis knew how cautious Amy was about showing people her work. She'd always been certain they would laugh or simply not understand her vision. Considering how unsupportive her parents were of her art, it was easy to understand why.

Her family hadn't lashed out physically at her the way his family had with him, but the wounds they'd inflicted were every bit as deep when they had barely glanced at her canvases before asking how her search for a *real* job was going.

He wished they could see that art wasn't just a hobby for her. But they'd made up their minds early on that art wasn't a serious, respected career path—not like banking or law. Was it any wonder that she was so nervous about showing her art to strangers?

Sure enough, when she returned from the parking lot with her painting in a tube under her arm, Travis saw her pause at the doorway, looking like a doe about to turn heel and run. Taking a deep breath, she lifted her chin, then headed for one of the tables covered in pressed linens.

Amy's hands shook slightly as she slid the canvas out. Travis wished he could reach out and hug her and let her know that she didn't need to be nervous around his friends. They weren't going to judge her.

"I thought giving Maya and Nolan a painting would be a little more special than just buying them a gift," she said. "I'm not sure the light is quite right in here...but, well, here goes."

She unrolled the canvas, and Travis's breath caught. Three years ago, Amy's talent had already been undeniable. But now?

He was completely blown away.

Her portrait was a stunning mixture of acrylics, pencil, and ink. Travis had seen photographs of both Maya and Nolan, and the likeness to the bride and groom in Amy's painting was excellent. But she had done so much more than just capture their features—she had brought their personalities to life. And since this was a surprise, she'd obviously done it without having them sit for the portrait.

"Your painting is amazing, Amy," Travis said.

"It really is lovely," Meg enthused. "Your use of color is fantastic. You've incorporated shades that most people wouldn't have thought to. I know exactly where it should be placed for the reception. Daniel, Jenn,

Nate!" Meg called out. "Come into the main hall. You need to see this."

Kate, meanwhile, had moved closer to study the painting more carefully. "How did you get that much rich pigment in the rose petals? They look so real."

Looking more than a little overwhelmed by everyone's response, Amy said, "I used pastels and then gloss varnished over them."

"How ever you did it," Kate said with a smile, "I almost feel as though I'm in a garden with real roses."

Travis was beaming with pride by the time Daniel and Jenn walked into the room, hand in hand.

"Nate is on another coffee run at the moment," Jenn told them, "and I've got bagels in the oven. But you don't normally yell, Meg, so I figured it must be important."

"It is," Meg assured them. "Come and look at this."

Kate reluctantly moved away from the painting so that Daniel and Jenn could see it.

"Wow," Jenn said, "this is absolutely beautiful."

Daniel studied it in silence for several long moments before finally looking up. "Did you paint this, Amy?"

Her cheeks were flushed as she nodded. "It's a wedding present for Maya and Nolan."

"They're very lucky," Daniel said. "You haven't just created a great likeness, you've told a story about their relationship and how much they mean to one another."

His expression was filled with admiration. "That's very hard to do."

Travis knew what high praise this was. Daniel was exacting about his craft and knew precisely the skill and artistry it took to capture a moment perfectly.

Liz was the only one who hadn't spoken yet. For the past several minutes, she'd been carefully studying the painting, her expression thoughtful. At last, she looked up and turned to Amy.

"Would you like to come work for us?"

Amy blinked at Liz, clearly stunned by her question. "You want *me* to work for *you*?"

"Yes, I would very much like for you to be Married in Malibu's official artist. I wouldn't want you to overlap with Daniel's photography, unless you both agreed that it made sense, but I believe our clients would absolutely love to have a unique and brilliantly painted portrait to remember their wedding by. Especially since it would be something they wouldn't be able to get at any other wedding venue. My goal is to make every Married in Malibu wedding utterly magical, and I'm certain that you would be an excellent addition to our team."

★ ★ ★

Amy stood frozen, not knowing what to say or do next. Being a portrait painter at Married in Malibu would be a dream come true.

But how could she accept when Travis worked here? Surely the last thing he wanted was to see her at work every day.

Her heart torn, Amy turned back to Liz. "Thank you for your offer. It sounds amazing. But—"

Liz held up a hand. "I understand that you need to focus on Maya's wedding for the next few days, but please tell me you'll at least take the time to think about my offer?"

In the face of such determination, Amy could say only one thing. "Okay, I will."

"Wonderful." Liz gave her another bright smile. "Now, if you will excuse me, I have to leave for a meeting. But please be sure to come find me if you have any questions or concerns about either the wedding or my offer."

"Come on," Travis said in a gentle voice as everyone headed back to work, "let's go get a cup of coffee. It will help."

Amy's head was spinning so much that she let Travis guide her outside and across the street toward a coffee shop, even though she should be keeping her distance.

"It's okay to feel a bit stunned," he continued in a low voice that soothed her even as it tempted. "She has that effect on people when she's trying to hire them. We all felt the same."

Inside the café, Nate was laughing with a woman

behind the register. As Amy and Travis made their way forward, she almost felt as though they were intruding on a private moment.

"Amy, this is Tamara. She owns Malibu T & Coffee. And of course, you've met Nate already, who drinks so much coffee every day that we're all amazed he doesn't bounce off the ceiling."

"Hey!" Nate protested. "I'm contributing to the local economy."

"Well, you are making up about half my profits at the moment." Tamara smiled over at them. "So what brings you here, Amy?"

"I'm the maid of honor for my friend's wedding." Amy knew better than to say *who* the wedding was for, in case anyone in the café was eavesdropping.

"She couldn't have picked a better venue," Tamara said. "Now, what can I get you to drink?"

This past year, Amy had been trying to keep away from the sweet stuff. But today, she desperately needed a hit of chocolate and sugar. "Is there any chance you could make me a mocha with chocolate sprinkles?"

"That sounds so good, I just might make one for myself," Tamara said as she got to work making the drink.

"I was wondering if you still drank that," Travis said.

"I've tried to give it up, but it's way too good." *Just like you.*

When his eyes darkened, she thought for a moment

she'd said the words aloud.

Fortunately, she hadn't. However, Tamara's gaze did sharpen on the two of them. "I thought it looked like you two knew each other."

Yet again, Amy was speechless. Because she certainly couldn't say to a woman she'd just met, *You're right. I fell in love with Travis three years ago. And then he broke my heart.*

Travis, however, didn't seem to have any trouble finding the right words. "We're old friends."

Amy whipped her head around to face him. *Old friends?*

How could he use such safe, tame words to explain what they'd been to each other?

Did old friends break each other's hearts?

Did they walk away without a second glance?

And did one old friend pine away for the other for three whole years?

Before Amy could say anything, he continued with, "Liz has offered Amy a job as Married in Malibu's portrait artist."

Nate's eyebrows lifted in surprise. "A lot happens when I go out to get coffee, doesn't it?"

"It was pretty sudden," Travis agreed, "but once you see Amy's painting of the bride and groom, you'll understand why Liz made her the job offer on the spot."

Amy's head continued to spin. Spending time with

Travis again was already more than enough to overload her system. Throw in Liz's job offer—and the fact that it actually sounded like Travis *wanted* her to take the job—and she honestly wasn't sure which way was up and which way was down anymore.

"Why don't you head over to the table in the corner?" Tamara said, as though she could see how badly Amy needed to sit down. "It has the best view of the ocean."

But Amy couldn't take in the blue waves or the surf. All she could hear was Travis saying *We're old friends* over and over inside her head.

"If you have any questions about Married in Malibu," he said once Tamara had brought over their drinks, "let me know. It's a great place to work. I know you'd love it."

At last, the dam inside Amy burst. "How can you sit there and talk to me about Liz's job offer like there's nothing wrong? Like it would be no big deal if we work together or not? Like we're nothing more than just *old friends*?" Warning bells were starting to chime inside her head. She was supposed to be holding it together. She was supposed to be cool. Calm. Collected. But she couldn't hold her feelings in anymore. "You broke my heart, Travis!"

For a long moment, he was silent. Finally, he said, "The last thing I ever wanted to do was hurt you." His words were softly spoken...and threaded with guilt. "You meant the world to me." He held her gaze, his expression seeming conflicted as he added, "You still do."

Her breath caught in her throat. Once upon a time, that was all she'd wanted—to mean the world to Travis. But though he claimed she still did, the fact was he'd walked away.

"If I meant so much to you—and if I still do—then why did you leave?"

Travis was a master of the impassive expression, never giving anything away. Which was why it had always touched her so much that he let his emotions run free when they were together. Now, however, she couldn't quite read what he was feeling. "All I've ever wanted is the best for you. I had to set you free."

"You thought pushing me away was the best thing you could do for me? You thought tearing us apart would set me free?" Didn't he understand that he'd torn her heart in two? "How could you possibly think that?"

Amy was surprised to see shame etched into his handsome face. "Because I'm not good enough for you."

"How can you say that?" Of all the reasons she'd thought he might give her, not being good enough for her wasn't anywhere on the list. "When we were together, you were always kind, generous, helpful, supportive. At least, until that day on the beach..."

"You don't know how sorry I am about what I did." He swallowed hard. "What I had to do, because of where I came from."

While they'd been dating, Travis had deliberately changed the subject whenever she'd tried to bring up his family. It had hurt that he hadn't wanted to share that part of himself with her, and she'd been too insecure about their relationship to press him on it. Now, however, she was not only older—and hopefully wiser—but she also wasn't afraid of what could happen if she pushed him too hard. Not when she'd already survived the worst. Well, mostly survived it, anyway.

"What is it, Travis? What could possibly be lurking in your past that's so bad?"

Of course, Nate had to choose that exact moment to come up to their table. "Sorry to interrupt, but Liz just texted. There's a problem with the feed for the security cameras, and I'm not sure if the issue is on my end or yours."

Travis jumped at the chance to get away. "Sorry about this, Amy, but I've got to make sure that the venue is secure."

She'd run from him last night. Now, he was the one making his way across the street as quickly as he could to get away from her.

# Chapter Five

Travis and Nate worked for several hours, heads bent over security cameras and computers as they dealt with the software update that had caused the wireless cameras and routers to stop communicating with one another. After Nate updated the protocols, Travis headed onto the grounds to restart the security cameras, one by one. Though he was glad the security system would soon be up and running at full speed, this also meant he had the mental space to think about Amy again—and about what she'd said at the coffee shop.

Not only that he'd broken her heart—which broke his all over again, just hearing her say the words—but also that she'd asked him to finally open up and tell her about his past.

When they were dating, he'd been so afraid of letting her see the darkness inside of him that he'd deliberately avoided telling her much at all. It wasn't lost on him that, though he was willing to take on just about any physical threat to keep clients safe, the thought of admitting the truth of his past filled him with dread. But now that she was here for the week—and possibly longer, if she agreed to Liz's offer—he knew he wouldn't be able to avoid answering her questions.

Once he told her everything, what would she do? Would she hate him the way he often hated himself? Would she want to get as far away from him as she could, even if it meant turning down the opportunity of a lifetime?

No, he couldn't let her do that. She deserved to be Married in Malibu's portrait painter. If anything, he would have to be the one to leave and find security work elsewhere. Surely Liz could replace him without too much trouble.

Knowing it was a conversation he should have had with his boss before now, he headed for Liz's office once he rebooted the last camera. Standing outside her door, he was more tempted to turn around and leave than he wanted to admit. Through sheer willpower, he forced himself to knock.

"Come in," Liz called. When Travis stepped inside, she said, "Hopefully, you're here to tell me that the security system is up and running again."

"We're back at one hundred percent," he assured her. "But I'm here to speak with you about something else." A major part of his job was making sure no surprises from people's pasts disrupted the weddings. His past with Amy was no exception. "It's about Amy and the job that you offered her."

"Don't you think it's a good idea?"

"I think it's a great idea. Amy is a very talented artist, and her painting of the bride and groom is going to be one of the highlights of the wedding. It's exactly the kind of chance that she deserves."

"Then what are you concerned about?"

Travis had always been extremely private about his personal life, and it wasn't any easier to get the words out than he'd thought it would be. "Amy and I have a history together, and I want to make sure it doesn't get in the way of either the wedding this weekend or Amy's chance to work here."

"How much history, exactly?"

"It's Amy's story as much as it is mine, so I don't want to go into all the details. But we used to be really close friends, until…" He paused to find the right words, but couldn't. He'd never known what to say to Amy either. "This is the first time we've seen each other in three years."

Liz's expression was thoughtful. "I imagine this must be quite difficult for both of you."

"It is," he admitted, "but Amy deserves this job. And I would never forgive myself if our past relationship held her back."

Liz got out of her seat and gestured for him to join

her by the window, which looked out over the gardens to the ocean beyond. Despite the difficult conversation they were having, he couldn't help but smile at Daniel and Jenn holding hands in the shade of a flowering tree.

"I had a similar conversation with Rose not so long ago," Liz said in a soft voice. "I was worried that she might not want to keep me on at Married in Malibu because of my past with Jason."

Liz and her new husband had broken up ten years earlier, only to be brought back together by his niece's wedding. Everyone was thrilled for them, including the co-owner of the wedding venue, Rose Knight.

Liz turned from the window to face him again. "If Amy does agree to work here, which I very much hope she will, I'm sure the two of you will find a way to work things out so that you're both happy, one way or another. After all," she said with a smile as she looked down at the wedding ring on her finger and then out the window at Jenn and Daniel, "finding happiness is what we do here at Married at Malibu."

* * *

By the time Amy returned to the rental house, Maya was there, looking absolutely gorgeous, even after her transatlantic flight. Her smooth, alabaster skin, startlingly blue eyes, and hair that flowed in waves to her shoulders made her features an artist's study in perfection. Amy had certainly sketched her enough times to know.

When Amy left the café, she had been surprised to find a message waiting on her phone from Maya, letting her know that she'd unexpectedly been able to cut her photo shoot short and was hopping on a fellow model's private plane to get here this afternoon. Nolan was on his way now, too.

After a big hug, Maya poured them two glasses of red wine, which they took over to the outdoor seating that overlooked the ocean.

Amy raised her glass for a toast. "To your wedding!" After they clinked and drank, she said, "You're going to love Married in Malibu. Everything about it is absolutely perfect."

One of Maya's brows arched in question. "Everything?" Only a best friend could get away with aiming straight at the heart of things after less than five minutes together. "Even seeing Travis again?"

Amy hated keeping anything from Maya, but she had made a vow to herself not to do anything to mess up her friend's wedding. What's more, she couldn't mention Liz's job offer, because that was directly linked to her secret wedding gift portrait. Which meant that she could give Maya only the abbreviated version of the past twenty-four hours.

"What I'm hearing," Maya said once Amy had finished speaking, "is that things are definitely not over between the two of you."

Though a secret bolt of hope jumped through Amy's heart, she said, "How can things 'not be over' when they never even really started?"

"It's one thing if it didn't start because he wasn't interested in you," Maya pointed out. "But he admitted today that all he wanted was the best for you and that you've always meant the world to him. Which I'm thinking is really good news, given that you're still in love with him."

"Still in love with him?" Maya's proclamation had Amy nearly spewing wine all over the outdoor couch. "I haven't even seen him for three years. I mean, he's been really nice since I've been here, but I'm—"

"Protesting far too much," Maya said with a gentle smile. "You don't have to pretend. I'm your friend, remember?"

"*Remembering* is exactly my problem right now," Amy said. "No matter how hard I try, I just can't seem to forget. Not any of it."

★ ★ ★

*Three years ago…*

Amy and Travis soon made it a weekend ritual to meet at the local farmers' market, grab a coffee, then walk along the beach. Though they hadn't officially started dating, she felt closer to him than she'd ever felt with anyone else.

Close enough that she started to wonder why they had never gone on an official date. In fact, the one time she had invited him back to her apartment for lunch, he'd told her he had a client waiting and that he had to leave.

She tried to be patient. Unlike other guys, who were out to take as much from her as quickly as they could get it, she hoped the fact that Travis was taking his time meant he was serious about getting to know her. And that he wanted far more than just a meaningless fling. Even so, Amy's patience had limits.

They had agreed to meet a little earlier one Saturday so that they could walk the beach before the farmers' market brought in the crowds. Her heart was pounding extra fast as she headed past the fruit and vegetable vendors setting up their booths, but she refused to wimp out. Not when she was absolutely certain about how good they could be together as more than just friends. When she found Travis standing with the sun at his back, any last nerves evaporated, her intentions feeling as pure and clear as the cloudless sky.

He turned just as she was running across the sand to him, his eyes wide as he took in the pretty sundress and makeup she'd put on especially for him.

"Amy? You look—"

She cut him off with a kiss. She had wanted to take her time, to start off sweet and gentle, but she'd been imagining what his lips would taste like almost from the first moment he had walked into the gym. Unable to help herself, she kissed him hungrily.

Finally, she pulled back, but only far enough to tell him, "I don't want to wait anymore. I don't want to take things slow. I'm in love with you, Travis."

In her dreams, she had been sure that he would tell her he felt the same way. Then he would return her kiss, and they would laugh at how long they'd both been wanting to confess their feelings to each other.

Instead, he stood perfectly still. Rigid, actually.

"Travis?" She hated the tremble in her voice. Hated the doubt that was quickly spreading through her as he gently removed her hands from around his neck and shook his head.

"I'm sorry, Amy. I can't."

She wasn't sure what he meant, just that every word he'd spoken had been colored with regret. "But I thought…? Don't you feel…? Aren't we…?"

"I can't," Travis said again. "Not with you."

Amy had never felt so foolish—or so hurt—in all her life.

* * *

*Present day…*

"Seeing Travis again is a bigger deal than I was ready for," Amy admitted to Maya. "But don't worry. I promised I'm not going to let anything ruin your wedding."

"I know you won't," Maya said. "But I'm not at all worried about that. I'm worried about *you*."

"I'm fine," Amy protested.

"Are you really?" She didn't wait for Amy to respond before adding, "Because I for one think that it's long past time for the two of you to talk. *Really* talk this time, without running when things get tough or scary."

If Amy was being honest with herself, she wanted that too. But what if Travis didn't?

The thought of putting herself out there again and being pushed away a second time was enough to make her chest ache. "I'm thrilled that you found your happy ever after, Maya. Unfortunately, that doesn't mean that the rest of the world gets one too."

"But what if you've *already* found your happy ever after?"

Amy loved Maya, but her friend could be like a dog with a bone. "Thank you for being there for me, like always, but what do you say we just focus on the wedding for now? After all, that's the real reason we're here. Not to try to get me and Travis together."

Maya was silent for a moment before nodding.

"Okay, then, how about we head over to Married in Malibu now to check things out? I know you've already been in today, but it's probably a good idea for you to be there with me to make sure I don't go all bridezilla on the staff. You know how we supermodels are," Maya said with a wink.

Amy laughed. "I can't even imagine it. You're one of the most mellow people I know." But she couldn't forget how serious Maya had looked when she'd said, *But what if you've* already *found your happy ever after?* "You're not going to do anything to try to get me and Travis back together, are you?"

"Don't worry," Maya replied. "If we see Travis, I'm not going to do anything crazy like lock you two in a room until you've worked everything out."

"Promise?"

Maya nodded, looking utterly angelic as she said, "I promise."

And yet, Amy wouldn't be at all surprised if Maya's promise was made with her fingers crossed behind her back.

# Chapter Six

Maya wasn't a bridezilla by any stretch of the imagination, but despite the information Amy had already given her, she did have a long list of questions for Liz and the others at Married in Malibu.

Fortunately, everyone was there except Travis, who was out picking up extra parts for a backup security system. For now, at least, there was no risk of Maya trying to get them together.

Which left Amy far more disappointed than she wanted to admit.

At present, Kate was giving Maya a comprehensive description of how she managed the flowers—she kept them growing at different stages throughout the year, chilled some to stop them from blooming too early and, if all else failed, had a half-dozen excellent suppliers on standby.

Amy appreciated how everyone at Married in Malibu had so much passion for their jobs, the same way that she did for her painting. If it weren't for how up in the air everything was with Travis—and how much she longed to see him, though it had barely been a handful of hours since they'd had coffee—accepting the job offer would have been a no-brainer.

At four p.m., Amy had an appointment to visit the teahouse where the bridesmaids would be gathering tomorrow afternoon. A half hour before, after letting Maya know where she was headed and being assured that someone on staff would drop Maya back at the rental house once they were finished with their meetings, Amy headed out.

As she drove through the back streets of Malibu, she tried to push away her churning thoughts so that she could enjoy the beautiful scenery. But no matter what she did, she couldn't stop thinking about Travis. And when the car suddenly made a bang and smoke started pouring from under the hood, she was so deep inside her head that she practically jumped out of her skin.

Trying not to panic, Amy carefully coasted the vehicle toward the side of the road, using the hand brake to slow it, then got out as soon as she deemed it safe. Wanting to put some distance between herself and the smoking vehicle, she moved into the shade of a large tree off the shoulder.

The road was several miles out of town, with barely any traffic at this time of the day, and what traffic there was rumbled past without slowing. Fortunately, Amy had enough bars on her cell phone to call the rental company, who told her they would send a tow truck and that they hoped to arrive within a half hour.

Silently telling herself everything was going to be fine—a phrase that had become a repeating chorus inside her head the past couple of days—she leaned against the nearest tree trunk, trying to no avail to get comfortable. Time had never passed so slowly before, and as she waited, she hoped that every vehicle around the bend would be the tow truck.

Twenty-five minutes into her wait, a big, black SUV drove past, then slowed and turned around before pulling in behind her car on the shoulder. Amy's heart rate jumped as she waited for the driver to emerge. Though she hoped the person was there to help rather than harm, she made sure to have 911 ready to call on her cell phone with just the press of her thumb.

When Travis stepped out, the wave of relief that hit her felt like being swept up in an ocean swell. Where before she'd felt frightened and vulnerable, now she felt utterly, completely safe.

Travis was here, and he would never let anything happen to her.

Perhaps it was a foolish way to feel considering how things had ended between them three years ago, but she felt it nonetheless.

She called out his name as she stepped out of the

trees, and he was quickly at her side, running his hands over her face and then her arms to make sure she wasn't hurt. "Are you okay? What happened?"

Warm all over from his touch, she said, "I was heading to the tea place where we'll be having the bridesmaids' reception tomorrow when the engine started making terrible noises and smoking."

"Thank God you're all right." He brushed his hand over her hair as though to reassure himself again. "Have you called a tow truck, or would you like me to take a look at?"

Before she could reply, the tow truck rounded the corner.

A few minutes later, she was in Travis's passenger seat, and they were on their way to the Mountain View Tea Shop.

Travis drove in the same way he did everything else, with quiet confidence, keeping his eyes on the road while also tracking well ahead for any potential problems. Amy could easily imagine him driving around a high-profile client, watching out for danger even as he kept the ride as smooth as possible.

The tea shop was exactly the way Amy had pictured it—a bright, lovely space set back in the hills—and so small that Travis looked like he would barely fit inside.

"I'm sorry I'm a little late," Amy said to the woman who greeted them. "I'm here about a booking for tomorrow. My name's Amy Woodford, and this is Travis."

"Ah, yes, I see it on my calendar." The woman smiled at both Amy and Travis. "Congratulations on your upcoming nuptials. It's always lovely to meet both the bride and the groom."

"Oh, no," Amy said quickly. "I'm afraid you have that wrong. It's for my friend's wedding, not mine. I'm her maid of honor. And Travis is—" *The man I once loved. And might still have feelings for, actually.* "—in charge of security at the wedding venue. My car just broke down on the side of the road, so he brought me here." She knew she was babbling, but that was because she was suddenly reeling from her sudden realization.

That she might still have feelings for Travis. Despite everything.

"In that case, I'm sure you'd like to sit down and relax a bit. I'll bring you a few things to taste, and then, if you'd like, you can make some changes to the menu for tomorrow."

Amy found herself ushered into a seat, while Travis perched on the dainty chair opposite hers. Was it just her imagination, or was everything in Malibu—from the weather to her rental car to the tea shop owner—trying to push them together?

"Well, that was awkward," Amy said as the woman hurried off to fetch cakes and tea.

"It's fine," Travis said.

But it wasn't. Couldn't he see that?

Just then, the owner returned with several teacups so that Amy and Travis could try a range of loose-leaf tea selections, along with a half-dozen delicate little cakes. Once they were alone again, Amy suddenly realized she had to take Maya's advice and talk to Travis. Really talk this time, when neither of them could run. Because she'd never be able to put things to rest inside her heart until she finally understood exactly what had happened between them.

"I've been thinking about what you said to me at the coffee shop," she began in a soft voice, "about how you deliberately kept your past from me." It wasn't easy to speak her feelings so plainly, but she made herself continue. "That hurt, Travis. So very much. Especially when I told you about things that were incredibly personal, and yet you didn't feel like you could trust me enough to do the same."

"Of course I trust you," he replied in a low voice. His hand closed around one of the cakes, tight enough that there were only crumbs left. "It's me I don't trust."

"*Please* tell me why you feel that way." Amy's voice trembled with emotion. "I promise that I would never judge you for anything you say or anything you've done."

\* \* \*

Travis had barely slept last night, thinking of how badly he kept hurting Amy by running out on her. Three years ago, he'd thought he was doing the right thing to protect her. But he'd only ended up hurting her. Only to hurt her again when he ran from her questions at the café.

"I don't know where to start." His whole career relied on him taking decisive action, knowing the right thing to do, and executing it before a situation could get out of hand. But with Amy, that point was long past. Still, he knew she deserved to hear more of his story. Enough, at least, that she might finally understand why he hadn't been able to let her think that he loved her—no matter what he'd really felt—and that she might also finally understand why she was better off without him.

"Growing up...things weren't good. It was a rough neighborhood, with a lot of bad things going on."

"What kind of bad things?"

"Gangs, drugs, fights."

"Are you trying to tell me that you were involved in all that?" Amy tilted her head to one side, looking at him carefully. "Because I have a hard time believing it when you're such a good person."

"I wasn't directly involved. But my family was. My mom died when I was young, so it was just me, my father, and my older brother."

"I didn't know that about your mom," Amy said. "I'm sorry."

She hadn't known because Travis hadn't dared to tell her even that much. He'd known that if he'd started talking about his past, the rest would have come out along with it.

"I never really knew my mom enough to miss her. But my father and my brother…" Travis paused to sip his tea, a momentary respite before he made himself continue. "They were monsters." Though Amy gasped at his language, there was no other word for it. "My dad was a drunk who only kept whatever his current job was until the boss figured out how worthless he was. My brother loved picking on, and fighting with, anyone smaller than him. I was smaller than him for a long time. I was smaller than them both."

"They hit you?" Amy asked, clearly horrified.

"Every day. Sometimes it would be one of them, sometimes the other. The bad days were the ones where they both decided it would be fun to remind me they were in charge." His father had owned a belt with metal studs that Travis could remember all too well.

"Travis." Amy reached across the table to put her hand over his. "Did anyone try to help? Did anyone in your neighborhood do anything to try to stop them from hurting you?"

"Eventually someone did." *He* had done what he had

to do to make sure that they would never hurt him again. "But for a long time, people just ignored it. Probably because all they saw was a kid who was destined to turn out exactly the same as his father and his brother. Worse, even, because he'd never known anything different."

"You turned out great!" Amy declared. "The person who saved you must have done a good job."

Travis swallowed hard. It was one thing to give her more details, but it was another to tell her absolutely *everything*. He still couldn't do that, not here in this tearoom when he knew she'd be so full of disgust that she'd need to get away any way she could, even if she had to walk back down the freeway to get home.

Instead, he told her a different truth: "I never saw love as a kid, so I didn't know what it looked like. Didn't even really believe it existed."

"You work at a wedding venue," Amy said with a gentle smile, "so you must know what love looks like by now."

She was right that Married in Malibu had a way of making a believer out of pretty much anyone. But the truth was that Travis learned what love looked like long before he took the job. From the first time he and Amy had walked and talked and laughed together—love had looked like *her*. But even now, he couldn't say it, couldn't risk dragging her into his life when she deserved so much more than him.

Thankful that he could finally shift the conversation away from his past, he said, "Married in Malibu definitely sees more than its fair share of couples who are deeply in love."

"Not to mention the way Jenn and Daniel look at one another."

Travis nodded, then told her, "Married in Malibu also brought Liz and her husband back together."

"It sounds like a truly magical place."

"It is. Which is why you should accept Liz's job offer. Not only will you be able to paint full time, but..." God, he hated to say the words, just as he hated to draw his hand away from hers. "Once you're back in Malibu, I'm sure you'll meet someone perfect for you. Someone who knows how to open up his heart all the way. Someone who isn't going to always screw things up or hurt you."

"Travis—"

The proprietor interrupted them before Amy could finish her thought. "I hope everything's all right? Are you enjoying the sample cakes and teas?" She gestured to the practically untouched plates in front of them. Amy had nibbled at the cakes, barely tasting anything. Travis hadn't touched his portions at all except to crumble the one cake in his fist. "Or would you like to try something else?"

"Everything is wonderful," Amy assured her hurriedly. "The bridesmaids are going to have a great time tomorrow. I don't need to sample anything else. Do you, Travis?"

"No," he said with a shake of his head, "and I should get you back. I know you've had a long day already."

After settling the bill, they headed out to his car in silence. He didn't know what else to say. More than anything, he wanted to be with her, but what could he do when he was still the same man? Still damaged. Still incapable of being everything Amy deserved.

It wasn't until he pulled into the driveway of her rental house that she finally spoke again. "Thank you for talking to me today, Travis. It means more than you know that you were willing to trust me."

And then she leaned over, kissed his cheek, and left him staring after her, wishing he could follow her and pull her into his arms. Wishing he could kiss her passionately. Wishing he could say that he'd fallen in love with her three years ago and had never stopped loving her.

Not for one single second while they were apart.

★ ★ ★

Amy's head—and heart—were both spinning faster than ever as she walked into the rental house.

"Whose car was that?" Maya asked. "What happened to your rental car?"

"It broke down, and Travis was passing when he spotted me. He took me to the tea shop, then gave me a ride home."

"That was Travis?" Maya hurried to the door as though she might still catch a glimpse of him. "The guy you're in love with was here and you didn't give me a chance to meet him?"

Amy smiled at that, but only a little. "You sound like you're my mother angling to find out if he's good enough for your little girl."

"Did I ever tell you that I actually got that from Nolan's mother? The first time we met, she gave me the third degree, asking if modeling could ever be a stable profession and whether she should expect to have paparazzi hiding in her flower beds."

Amy would normally have laughed at that story. When she didn't, Maya reached out to put a hand on her shoulder. "Something more happened with Travis than just a busted car engine and a visit to the tearoom, didn't it?"

"You're supposed to be getting ready for your wedding," Amy deflected. "Surely there's something you want to talk over with me after your meetings today."

"Married in Malibu has everything under control, and my wedding is going to be perfect." Maya inclined her head toward Amy. "Now that we've gotten that out of the way, you can tell me about what happened with

Travis this afternoon over a glass—or two—of bubbly."

Maya grabbed a bottle of champagne and two glasses, then gently pushed Amy out onto the deck that overlooked the beach.

"Now," Maya said once they each had a glass in hand, "what did he do that has you so flustered?"

Amy looked out over the ocean and took a deep breath of salty air before replying, "I took your advice and asked him to talk to me. Really talk this time. And he ended up telling me about his past. Some of it, anyway."

She was glad that he had finally opened up to her. And yet, she couldn't push away the sense that he'd filled in his backstory the way a painter might lay down the initial coats of paint on a canvas, in broad washes of color that hadn't yet acquired real form. Creating a painting that wasn't anywhere near finished yet.

"What happened to him?" Maya asked.

Amy shook her head. "I can't give you the details. Only he can, if he ever chooses to. But what I can tell you is that, though he hasn't done anything wrong, his life *definitely* hasn't been easy or fair. Which just makes everything he's achieved, everything he is, even more impressive."

"And now that he's shared his past with you?"

That was the part Amy was still trying to work out. Why did he think that having a bad history, no matter what had happened to him, would change anything about the way she felt for him?

Why had he felt he needed to walk away three years ago, rather than simply telling her all of this in the first place?

And why couldn't she stop thinking about him? Couldn't stop her heart from racing whenever he was near? Couldn't stop wanting to throw herself into his arms and kiss him? Couldn't help but feel safe with him, despite how conflicted she was inside her heart.

Again, she felt find a tiny hint of hope glimmering inside her. Travis hadn't left because he found someone else, or because he didn't love her. He'd left because he hadn't thought he was good for her.

When the truth was that he was the best man she'd ever known.

She took a large gulp from her glass, and maybe it was the champagne talking, but she couldn't keep her hopes to herself another second. "I can't believe I'm about to say any of this, but now that Travis has finally started to open up, I'm thinking about giving him another chance." Bumping Maya's shoulder with her own, she added, "This is the part where you tell me that I'm being completely insane to even consider giving a second chance to a guy who broke up with me before we even started officially dating."

Only instead of confirming that she'd lost her marbles, Maya said, "True love is the best thing in the whole wide world. I couldn't imagine what my life would be like if I weren't marrying Nolan. Whereas you *have* gotten to see what life is like without Travis—and we both know how much you missed him. So now that you've got a second chance, if you think that he's your one true love, then honestly, there's only one thing I can tell you right now."

Amy's heart was in her throat as she said, "What's that?"

Maya put her arm around Amy, then said, "You have to take a chance on true love with Travis again. Or you'll regret it for the rest of your life."

# Chapter Seven

Late the following afternoon, Travis cursed his efficiency, as thoughts of Amy were waiting just on the other side of his security preparations for the wedding, which were now complete.

Needing to find more to do or risk his feelings for Amy overwhelming him, he headed for Liz's office. The door was closed, and as he knocked, he heard laughter from within, followed by, "Come in."

Travis wasn't surprised to find Jason inside. The famous thriller writer often came over when he was done with his morning's writing to take his wife to lunch. Both Liz and Jason had the slightly guilty looks of people caught out at more than picking which restaurant to go to.

"My security preparations are finished," Travis said, "so I thought I'd check to see if you needed any extra help with anything."

"I'm all set on my end," Liz replied, "but Daniel is setting up a backdrop for photographs in the garden, so perhaps you could see if he needs a hand. Preferably before Nate decides to give up on coding the lighting sequences to work on it."

Travis smiled in silent agreement that their computer expert did rather seem to prefer working with his hands and a hammer.

Down in the garden, Daniel had laid backboards and reflectors along the garden path. Kate was hovering just on the other side of the garden, shooting worried looks at Daniel, obviously ready to pounce at the slightest hint of damage to her plants. Jenn was there too, clearing up what looked like an old-fashioned picnic in the garden, complete with blanket and hampers.

"What's this?" Travis asked.

"I thought it would be nice to add something informal into the wedding," she explained. "While I was waiting for some dough to rise, I thought I'd take the time to experiment."

A new element to the wedding reception meant a new set of potential security concerns. Fortunately, after some quick mental calculations, Travis decided his existing security arrangements would easily cover it.

"I like how you're always coming up with new and innovative ideas, Jenn," Travis said.

"I do too," Daniel agreed, walking over to put an arm around her and giving her a kiss on her forehead before she headed back to her kitchen to put her bread in to bake.

Normally, the fact that everyone was in a kissing mood would have been just fine with Travis. Today, however, it served only as a reminder of the fact that he couldn't kiss Amy...no matter how bad he wanted to.

"I can lend a hand with backdrop construction if you need it, Daniel."

"I could definitely do with an extra pair of hands so that I don't risk Kate's wrath by damaging any of the flowers."

"Even I couldn't protect you from that," Travis said as they moved the screens and the reflectors for the backdrop into place, then bolted them down.

"So, how are things going?" Daniel asked. "I don't want to pry, and you should feel free to tell me to get lost, but I get the sense something's weighing on you."

Travis always made sure to keep his feelings inside. But now that Amy had appeared back in his life from out of the blue, his hold on his emotions was shakier than it had ever been.

"I'm worried about a friend of mine," he finally said. "She's so smart and talented that the world should be at her feet."

"But?"

Travis shook his head. "It's complicated."

Daniel nodded. "I know more than my fair share about complicated."

After working together for several months, Travis knew Daniel's story—he'd lost his wife in a terrible accident, then given up his award-winning photojournalism career to be a stay-at-home father for his children. Finding Jenn—and falling in love—had given him a second chance at life.

"I'm sure you're doing everything you can to help your friend," Daniel continued.

Travis had thought that was exactly what he'd done for Amy three years ago, but he'd only ended up hurting her. That was unforgivable enough.

But what if she turned down the opportunity to work at Married in Malibu because he worked there?

"I haven't done everything I can to help her." Travis's voice was full of anger—at himself. "Not by a mile."

Daniel stopped screwing in a bolt to look at Travis. "That doesn't sound like you."

"What do you mean?"

"You're one of the most helpful people I know. There isn't anyone you won't bend over backward to assist. Which is why I'm finding it hard to believe that you haven't already bent over backward for your friend."

"I haven't," Travis insisted.

"Well, then, could you now? I don't know what field your friend is in, but you've worked as a bodyguard for so long, I'm guessing you must know people in pretty much every line of work."

Daniel was right that Travis had done security for a Who's Who of Los Angeles, from producers to actors, singers to artists. Art collectors too.

"You know what…" An idea began to take shape. "I just might know the perfect person."

He might not be able to convince Amy to take the job at Married in Malibu—and he certainly couldn't change his past—but he could introduce her to Johan Vanderwol, an extremely influential gallery owner and art collector. Travis had stopped one of Johan's paintings from being slashed last year, and Johan had reacted as though Travis had saved his firstborn.

As soon as Daniel's set was completely in place, Travis headed back to his office to make the call. Johan picked up on the first ring. "Travis, great to hear from you. How are things?"

"Great, thanks." He hated asking for favors, but there was nothing he wouldn't do for Amy. "Do you remember when you said if I ever needed anything, all I had to do was call?"

"Of course. Anything I can do for you, just name it."

"There's an artist I'd like for you to meet with. Amy Woodford. I'm not asking you to buy her work, or host a show for her, but if you could take a look at her paintings, it would mean the world to her." He paused before adding, "And to me."

"We're having a showing for a local artist tonight," Johan said. "Why don't you ask Amy to come by and say hello?"

After thanking Johan, Travis dialed Amy's cell. He hadn't needed to look up the number—not when he still remembered it by heart. So many times over the past three years, he'd nearly called her, just to hear her voice. Now, he finally had a reason to call.

"Is everything okay for the wedding?" she asked when she picked up. "I've just returned from tea with Maya's bridesmaids, and I didn't think to check my phone until now."

"Don't worry, nothing's wrong. The opposite, in fact. I just got off the phone with a guy I know who runs an art gallery downtown. They're having a show to-night, and I mentioned you. He'd like for you to come by and introduce yourself."

"You...you did that for me?"

"Of course I did." He wished she knew that he'd do anything for her.

"I'd love to go," Amy said. "Thank you so much for calling him on my behalf." There was a short pause, and then she asked, "Will you go with me to introduce us in person?"

Travis had been thinking only of how good it would be for Johan to see Amy's paintings. But now that she had asked him to join her, despite knowing better than to keep putting himself in the path of temptation, there was only one response he could give her.

"I would love to."

# Chapter Eight

The gallery was incredibly impressive, one of the top art spaces in Los Angeles. So impressive, in fact, that people were lining up outside to get in. Amy could barely believe the owner actually wanted to talk to *her*.

Travis was wearing a dark suit that made it hard for her not to stare and drool over how handsome he was. She'd done her best to dress for the occasion by borrowing one of Maya's cocktail dresses, and it had been well worth squeezing into it just to hear Travis say she looked beautiful when he came to pick her up. Thankfully, Maya had been out, or she would have surely given him the third degree.

He led the way to the door, ignoring the line. The security staff waved them through, giving him nods of recognition as they passed.

"You know them?" she guessed.

He nodded. "I've worked with them before."

Inside, the gallery had used lighting and mirrors to optimize each work of art. Men in expensive suits and women whose dresses surely hadn't been borrowed from a friend stood chatting, champagne glasses in hand. Quite a few of the latter seemed to be looking at Travis instead of the art, obviously wishing they could take him home instead.

"Hello, Travis." The woman who had come up to them was not only beautiful and well dressed, but her jewelry alone must be in the six figures. Amy thought she looked familiar, but she couldn't imagine where they might have met in the past. "It's lovely to see you again."

"Hello, Helen," Travis replied in a friendly but not at all obsequious way. "Good to see you. This is Amy Woodford."

He didn't say that she was an *old friend* this time, and guilt pricked her at how she'd ripped into him for it at the café. If only she'd understood then how conflicted he was over his past.

"It's lovely to meet you, Amy." Helen's smile was friendly, which helped put Amy more at ease. Turning back to Travis, the woman asked, "Are you here running security for someone? Or to pick up some art?"

"Neither. Amy's an artist, and Johan would like to meet with her."

"Wonderful," Helen said. "I hope we'll see your work hanging here soon, Amy."

It was only after the woman had walked away that Amy realized where she'd seen her before. Helen

Polland had been in so many movies that seeing her in real life was more than a little surreal. Travis, on the other hand, treated chatting with a major movie star like it was no big deal.

As they made their way through the gallery, plenty of other movie and TV stars, musicians, and athletes came up to Travis to chat as though greeting an old friend. For the first time, Amy understood just how famous his clientele had been. Whether he was speaking with a director whose latest movie was a box office smash or a rapper with a massive business empire, Travis was perfectly relaxed. Meanwhile, Amy had to work at not embarrassing herself by fangirling all over the stars.

"Are you doing okay?" Travis asked her as they headed up the stairs and toward the back of the building.

"I'm a little overwhelmed," Amy said. And not only because of all the star power in the gallery.

Amy couldn't help but compare the art in the gallery to her own work—and what she saw had her feeling more worried by the moment. The paintings on display were so powerful, with such bold use of color and such clear emotion.

Was there any way she could ever belong here?

On top of that, being so close to Travis again tonight—every time he put his hand on the small of her back to guide her through the crowd, her whole body heated up—she had to exert every ounce of control not to throw herself into his arms and beg him to kiss her.

"Don't be nervous." Travis reached out to touch her arm, giving her the comfort she so badly needed but also inadvertently setting off more sparks inside of her. "Johan is going to love your paintings. You're every bit as good as these other artists. Better, if you ask me."

Without Travis by her side, Amy might have turned and run rather than brave meeting the man at the center of all of it, directing the party the way a conductor might direct an orchestra. Did Travis have any idea how much she'd always appreciated his support?

Johan, wearing a bespoke suit, had sandy-blond hair that fell to his shoulders. He smiled at Travis. "Glad you could make it." He turned to Amy, holding out his hand. "You must be Amy. Travis neglected to tell me you were so lovely."

"Easy, Johan," Travis said mildly when Johan held on to her hand a few moments longer than was strictly polite.

As soon as the gallery owner let go, Travis put an arm around her shoulders...and the glimmer of hope inside Amy did a small twirl at his obviously jealous reaction to Johan's flirting.

"Thank you so much for agreeing to meet with me," Amy said, trying not to stutter over her words in nervousness.

"After Travis and I spoke, I looked up some of your work. What I saw was quite good." The blood rushing in her ears made it hard for her to hear him add, "Perhaps you could bring me a few paintings to see in person later this week?"

"Of course I can!" Her voice was a little too high-pitched, borderline squeaky, but she couldn't help it. Not when this was *far* more than Amy had hoped might come out of the evening.

"I'm sorry I can't speak more with you tonight." Johan gestured to the party. "But be sure to call me to set up a time to meet. And don't be a stranger, Travis."

Once Johan had gone, and they'd left the crowded gallery to get some fresh air, Travis said, "That seemed to go well, didn't it?"

"I can't believe how well it went!" She couldn't keep from throwing her arms around him—just as she couldn't help but relish every precious moment in his arms. "Thank you so much for contacting him on my behalf."

"It's the least I could do." His expression was so serious, and she wanted nothing more than to kiss it away. "I wish I had been a better friend to you these past years, Amy. I'm so sorry that I wasn't."

She pressed a finger to his lips. "I'm not thinking about the past anymore. You shouldn't either. The only thing that matters is right now."

Above them, the moon was full, shining shafts of light down onto the water so that it seemed more silver than dark blue. The night was perfect, cloudless without being cold, the stars above just right.

And it suddenly seemed the most natural thing in the world to replace her finger on his lips with a kiss that tasted even more perfect than she remembered.

Only this time, Travis kissed her back.

*Thank God.*

Wrapping his arms around her, he held her tightly against him as their kiss spun on and on, growing more passionate by the second. Standing in the gallery's garden space, which was getting more crowded by the second, they had to stop kissing too soon and move apart.

Staring at each other in silence, Travis didn't seem to know what to say or do next. That was fine, though, because after a kiss that had been both sweet and sinful, Amy didn't exactly know either.

All she knew for sure right now was that she'd never felt more hopeful.

And that she'd never been more in love.

*Chapter Nine*

The next day, Amy couldn't stop smiling while she and Travis worked together to hang her painting of Maya and Nolan. She'd been worried that things might be awkward in the aftermath of their unexpected kiss, but if anything, Travis seemed more at ease with her than before.

Almost as though their kiss had broken the ice that had built up between them over the past three years.

Not, of course, that either of them had actually *talked* about the kiss. Maybe, she thought with another smile, talking was overrated, and they should just stick to kissing for a while...

"Does that look right?" Travis lifted her painting into position as carefully as he would a Van Gogh or a Matisse.

"It looks perfect from where I'm standing," Amy assured him, and she didn't just mean the picture. But she didn't want to say too much, too quickly. Not when what was growing between them again felt so fragile and precious—and she didn't want to make the mistake of rushing things the way she had before.

Just as Liz had promised, the Married in Malibu workshop had been well equipped with everything they needed to frame her painting. She had chosen a relatively simple wooden frame design, then painted it to match the colors of the wedding backdrop.

"If you could hold it still for another couple of seconds," he said, "I'll get the last hangers in the wall."

Though he was pounding the hammer just inches from her fingers, Amy felt perfectly safe. There was no one else she would have trusted as much with her hands, or the painting she had worked so hard on. Only Travis.

They had just finished hanging the painting and covering it with dark, velvet fabric Meg had embroidered around the edges for an elegant touch when Liz brought in a stack of beautifully wrapped wedding gifts.

"These have been collecting all week, and I was thinking the perfect spot for them is on the table beneath your painting, Amy."

After Liz had artfully arranged the gifts, then headed back to her office, Amy turned to Travis. "I'm sure this wasn't what she intended, but the setup makes it look like my gift is the most important one here."

"That's because it is," he replied. "Your painting is going to wow everyone here, most especially the bride and groom. It's absolutely breathtaking."

In that moment, she could have sworn that the look he gave her said the painting wasn't the only thing there he found breathtaking. And when Travis looked at her like that, it was hard not to think that maybe, just maybe, things might work out for them this time.

★ ★ ★

"Thanks for standing in for Maya and Nolan," Nate said from his digital command center. Above Travis and Amy, the lighting rig flickered to life. "It's so hard to get the spotlighting correct without an actual couple on the dance floor."

Travis couldn't help but be pleased when Amy had agreed to dance with him in the middle of the reception hall this afternoon. Nor could he stop wishing Nate's casual use of the word *couple* could actually become real for them, even if there must surely be a man out there who would be better for Amy.

As he drew her close, he remembered how good kissing her had felt last night...and thought how easy it would be to lean in just that little bit more to kiss her again.

"Just keep doing what you're doing," Nate called out, momentarily breaking the spell. "A slow dance is the perfect speed for me to calibrate the lights."

As the music played on and they continued to sway together, Travis simply didn't have the will to deny himself the pleasure of being so close to her. Especially when her lips brushed against his neck, soft and delicate—and more than enough to drive Travis wild with longing.

When the music stopped, it took him a handful of beats to notice. His security career hinged on paying close attention to his surroundings, but when Amy was near, she was the only thing that mattered.

"Would you like to get dinner tonight?" The words came before he could hold them back, just as they had the night she'd surprised him by showing up in the rain.

Only today, instead of running away, she gave him a smile that was brighter than any spotlight could ever be as she nodded and said, "I would love to."

★ ★ ★

They found a cozy restaurant with a corner booth where they could talk about everything and nothing. Though their meals were delicious—Amy had the vegetable sauté, while Travis opted for steak—what they ate didn't matter.

All that mattered was how natural it felt when he reached across the table to take her hand...and how wonderful it was to be with him again.

Three years ago, when she had thrown herself at him on the beach, he'd panicked, deciding it was better to send her running than tell her about his past. Tonight, however, she not only had much better insight into his heart—but she also couldn't stop thinking about what Maya had said. *You have to take a chance on true love with Travis again. Or you'll regret it for the rest of your life.*

She barely tasted her desert, too busy looking across the table at him. Too busy thinking about how much she loved being with him. Too busy thinking about how much she wanted him.

When they finally finished their meal, she was mustering up her bravery to say she didn't want to go back to the beach house just yet, but Travis beat her to it.

"Come home with me, Amy."

It was the most natural thing in the world to go.

\* \* \*

Travis could see Amy taking in the details of his house with her artist's eye—the leather couches and wood furniture, gifts given from grateful former clients, photographs of some of the exotic locales he'd visited as a bodyguard. They weren't so much memorabilia as reminders that he'd done his job well and kept people safe. It was strange to think that this was the first time she'd been in his home.

"I like your house," she said. "It's warm and handsome, just like you."

She turned to kiss him, and Travis caught her up in his arms, kissing her back eagerly. But it wasn't enough just to show her how much she meant to him—he needed to tell her too. Needed her to know what had been inside his heart for three long years.

"I love you, Amy."

Her eyes grew wide, then filled with joy. "Do you know how long I've been waiting to hear you say that?"

"I'm sorry—"

She put her finger to his lips. "Don't apologize. Just say it again."

"I love you."

"I love you too." She kissed him deeply, passionately. Then drew back enough to say, "Take me to bed, Travis. We've waited long enough, don't you think?"

Maybe he still wasn't good enough for her. Maybe he never would be.

Tonight, though, he wasn't strong enough to let that stop them from loving each other.

He swept her up into his arms and carried her into his bedroom.

★ ★ ★

A long while later, Amy lay in the dark, wrapped in Travis's arms, relishing every perfect moment of their lovemaking. After waiting for so long, being with him had been even sweeter, even more passionate and perfect than she could have ever imagined.

Especially now, when she'd never felt so safe or so

happy.

Loving the warm strength of his body against hers, Amy pressed closer to Travis, smiling as she drifted toward sleep.

*Chapter Ten*

Every single second since Amy had woken up in his arms, Travis felt as though he had been holding his breath, watching for even the slightest sign that she was uncomfortable or unsure about their lovemaking...or the vows of love they'd made to each other.

Thankfully, she had been full of smiles and laughter all morning—and so sweetly seductive that Travis would have happily stayed in bed with her all day were it not for the bride and groom waiting for them at Married in Malibu.

Yet, his nerves still wouldn't settle. Not when, in his heart of hearts, he remained a long way from believing that he could ever be worthy of her love.

Travis was usually the first one on-site at Married in Malibu. Today, however, he and Amy arrived after everyone else, including the bride and groom.

He'd been bracing himself for meeting Maya. Surely Maya would take one look at him, see that he wasn't good enough for her best friend, then set Amy up with a movie star.

But when Amy introduced them, Maya couldn't have been friendlier as she shook his hand and said, "It's great to finally meet you, Travis." In fact, if he wasn't mistaken, Maya actually looked *pleased* to see him and Amy together.

Nolan shook his hand next. "Thank you for helping put on our wedding. We couldn't have asked for a better venue."

"We really couldn't have," Maya agreed. "And your timing is perfect, Amy, because Jenn has made a whole array of petits fours, and I need your opinion on which to serve at the reception." Somehow, Travis doubted that would be the only thing they were going to talk about, especially given that whatever Maya whispered to Amy as they walked away had Amy's cheeks growing even rosier.

"If you don't mind," Nolan said, "I'd be interested in getting a look at your security setup."

Maya's fiancé was a surprisingly normal guy. With light brown hair and a conservative gray suit, he looked like he belonged in an office, rather than on a runway or in a movie studio.

Travis led the way, explaining the security considerations as they made their way across the property. "The main balancing act is giving the guests total access to the grounds and the beach cove without allowing any uninvited photographers or press to get inside."

"That explains all the cameras."

"Exactly," Travis said, before delving deeper into the cutting-edge security technology. A quick study, Nolan asked plenty of good questions, and before Travis knew it, they had covered the grounds from the beach to the garden.

Through the windows of the kitchen that looked out onto the grounds, Travis could see Amy and Maya laughing with Jenn as all three licked cake and frosting off their fingers.

"I'm really glad Amy is here to help out," Nolan said. "There isn't a contract on the planet that can throw me, but when it comes to linens and place markers, I'm completely lost."

"That's what we're here for," Travis reassured him.

"I know you are, and I appreciate it more than you know. I just..." Nolan ran a hand through his hair, clearly worried about something. "Maya deserves everything in this wedding to be as perfect as she is, and I keep worrying that there's something more I should be doing."

Travis could understand that feeling all too well. Whenever he was with Amy, he wanted to make the world a better place simply so that she would be happy. "You want to keep her safe—and give her absolutely everything."

"That's it exactly. But sometimes…" The other man looked bleak. "Sometimes, I still can't believe that she picked me. Maya could have any man she wanted, so how did I get so lucky? And how can I ever make sure I'm giving her everything she needs and deserves?"

It was so close to how Travis had always felt about Amy that he found himself saying, "You end up feeling that you can never be good enough. You look at her and know that she deserves so much more than you can give. You're more in love with her than ever, but it's not about what you want, it's about what she deserves. And she deserves everything in the world. If you could give it to her on a silver platter, that might just be enough. But you know that you never can."

It took several long moments for Travis to realize what he'd said. He shouldn't be talking through his personal problems with clients, especially the fiancé of Amy's best friend. Unfortunately, Travis had gotten so lost in his conflicted emotions that he hadn't been able to properly do his job.

"Nolan, I apologize for speaking out of turn like that." He couldn't let Nolan go on such a down note. Liz would kill him if the groom got cold feet, and rightly so. "You and Maya wouldn't be on the verge of getting married if you weren't great together. Amy has said more than once what a great couple you are."

"That's good to hear," Nolan said in response to

Travis's pathetic attempt to smooth things over. When his fiancée saw them and waved, the groom seized the opportunity to get the heck out of there. "Thanks for the tour, but we should probably get back inside. Looks like Maya needs me."

\* \* \*

Amy was having the time of her life helping Maya with the last-second wedding details, from choosing the right dessert cakes to solving a sudden seating snafu. It helped that Married in Malibu was such a well-oiled machine, and of course, there was nothing Amy wouldn't have done to support her best friend in creating the most memorable day of her life. At the same time, Amy couldn't deny that the biggest reason she couldn't stop smiling today was her budding relationship with Travis. Not to mention their super-sexy night.

Maya kept pressing her for details, but though the two women usually shared everything with each other, Amy wanted to privately savor the intimate hours she and Travis had spent together.

"Watching you and Travis come back together after all these years," Maya said as they were leaving the kitchen arm in arm, "makes me believe in the power of love even *more* than I already did."

"I'm pretty sure spending time around all the beautiful wedding cakes and decorations at Married in Malibu makes *everyone* believe in the power of love," Amy teased, even though she was feeling the same way.

She was feeling so positive about how things were going with Travis, in fact, that she was tempted to go find Liz right now to say that she would happily take the job at Married in Malibu. Only the fact that she needed to keep her painting a secret from Maya made her hold off.

Nolan came inside, and Maya immediately went to put her arms around him. "Want to taste the cakes we chose?"

"Anything for you," Nolan said. The two of them left Amy in the hall just as Travis walked in.

Though they'd been apart for only a half hour, seeing him again made Amy light up from the inside out. Just as Maya had with Nolan, she wanted to put her arms around the man she loved and know that nothing would ever tear them apart.

But the look on his face—no smile, just that tic he got in his right cheek whenever he was clenching his teeth—made her nervous. Nervous enough that she found herself trying to make small talk to fill the suddenly uncertain space between them.

"Nolan is a great guy, isn't he?"

"He is," Travis said. But he was frowning. And she couldn't miss the sadness in his eyes—the same expression he'd had when he talked about his past.

Waking up in Travis's bed this morning hadn't been awkward at all. On the contrary, it had felt perfectly right. Their conversation had been easy and comfortable as they'd driven to Married in Malibu. Even when he'd met Maya, everything had seemed perfectly fine.

Until now.

"Travis?" Amy moved closer, though his body language was telling her to keep her distance. "What is it?"

He was silent for a long moment. Long enough that she was certain her heart would race all the way out of her chest. "I'm sorry, Amy. I thought I could do this. But...I can't."

"Can't do what?" She could barely breathe, barely get the words out.

"This." The one word fell like a blade between them. "Us."

# Chapter Eleven

"What do you mean, you can't do it?" Amy kept her voice quiet, as though she might set off an avalanche otherwise. "After last time, I thought—"

"That's just it. Nothing has changed since the last time I left you. I'm still the same guy I was then, and last night I was fooling myself when I thought we could be together."

This couldn't be happening again. It just couldn't. "Before you left, everything was going great. *We* were going great." Her head was spinning. Her heart was too, but not in a good way. "Tell me what you and Nolan talked about in the last thirty minutes to change your mind."

"This has nothing to do with Nolan. This is about me not being strong enough to keep from wanting to be with you, even though I know I still don't deserve you."

"Don't I get any say in that?" She couldn't keep her voice from rising.

"I'm not good for you. I'm not safe for you to be

around."

"I've never felt as safe with anyone as I do with you, Travis." How could she possibly get him to understand? "I know your family treated you horribly, but you rose above them."

"No, I didn't." He stood as impassive as a statue. "I'm no good."

"How can you say that you're no good? What they did to you wasn't your fault."

"You don't understand."

It was obvious that he wanted to leave it at that, but she couldn't let him. Not this time. "*Make* me understand."

When he didn't speak for several long moments, she feared he would shut her down again. But then his face fell even more, and he finally said, "For so many years, they beat on me and beat on me. They just assumed that I would always be smaller, always be weaker. Every time they hit me, it felt like I didn't have any control over my life or my body, so I started to take control. I ran, and I lifted weights. I wrestled in high school, and I played football. By the time I was eighteen, I was bigger than both of them. And yet, they still felt like they could hurt me whenever they wanted to." He took a deep breath before continuing, and she could hear it shake inside his chest. "One day, I'd had enough, and I...snapped. I gave them the kind of beating they'd been giving me and more." His words were coming out in agonized bursts. "I saw red, and by the time I came back to myself, they were both on the ground bleeding and begging me to stop, and my fists were raw."

She reached for him, desperate to soothe his pain. "Travis—"

He backed away before she could touch him. "The worst part wasn't looking at them afterwards. It wasn't seeing their fear, seeing how frightened they were of me, just like I had been scared of them." He swallowed hard. "The worst part was that even knowing the pain I'd caused them, I knew that if they ever put me in that same situation, I would do it all over again." Her heart broke a million times over for him as he said, "How could you ever love a man like that?"

"Easily." He blinked at her as though he couldn't believe her response. "You were on the receiving end of horrible pain for a very long time." She wanted so badly to make him see the truth. "You acted in self-defense. They would have kept hurting you if you hadn't fought back."

"But if you had seen me that day…" She had never seen him look so bleak. Or so broken. "No one could love a man capable of doing what I did. No one *should* love a man with such rage inside him. Inside," he pounded his fist against his chest, "I'm a monster."

"How can you think that when every time you've

touched me, every time you've held me, every time you look at me, you're so gentle, so wonderful, so loving?" Her eyes were wet with tears. "You're not a monster, Travis. You're the best man I know."

Only, he didn't seem to hear her as he said, "When you came back this week, I wanted to believe things could change—that *I* could change and be that better man you think you see. But the truth is that if I had to go back to that room with my father and brother, even knowing what I know now, I would do the same thing. Nothing has changed, Amy. Nothing at all."

Three years ago, Amy had let her heart be broken. She had run from the hurdles love threw in her way, rather than standing her ground and fighting for happiness. Now, it would be so easy to do the same thing—to give up, to get on a plane back to Michigan and try to forget the only man she had ever loved.

But Amy was older now. Wiser. And a heck of a lot stronger.

"You're right," she said. "Nothing has changed." She took a step toward Travis, catching his hands in hers before he could stop her. "Nothing has changed, because I still love you. And I know you love me too, even if you're too stubborn to admit it. But I'm not going to run away this time and lick my wounds. Instead, I'm going to be right here, waiting for you to stop being so stubborn. Waiting for the moment when you wake up and look in the mirror and realize a monster has never been staring back at you. Waiting for you to realize that you deserve not only to be loved, but to give love with your whole heart. To love me the same way I love you. Unconditionally."

★ ★ ★

"Amy?"

Maya called out her name as she shot past Married in Malibu's kitchen a short while later, but Amy didn't stop. She was desperate to get out of the building before anyone saw her crying.

Of course, her friend soon tracked Amy down on a bench beneath a tree in a back corner of the garden. "What's wrong?" Maya sat and put an arm around her. "What happened?"

"You should be with Nolan right now." Amy wiped her eyes dry with the back of her hand. "You're getting married tomorrow. You don't have to worry about me."

"I'm your best friend and I love you. So that means whenever you need me, I'm going to be there for you." Maya waited until Amy met her gaze. "Now, talk to me."

"Last night, Travis told me he loved me." And his words of love had meant absolutely everything to her, especially after she had waited so long to hear them. "But now he says that he still doesn't believe I could possibly love him, because he doesn't believe he's worthy of being loved by *anyone*." She'd never felt so emotional, not even after Travis had spurned her on the beach three years ago. "I've told him I'm going to wait for him to see the truth—but will I ever be able to convince him that I really, truly do love him and that he really, truly is worthy?"

Maya looked pensive, her gaze trained on the ocean beyond the gardens for several long moments. Finally, she said, "I wish I had a simple answer for you." She sighed. "I know this isn't easy to hear, but maybe if it's this hard to get him to come around, you shouldn't wait for him."

"You can't actually mean that!" Amy was shocked that Maya would even suggest it. "That would be like asking you to give up Nolan. Plus, *you* were the one who said I should give true love a second chance."

"First, I would never give up Nolan, no matter how big the bumps in the road might be," Maya confirmed. "And second, of course I don't actually mean it."

"Wait a minute," Amy said, her head spinning again. "Did you just say that so I would realize I'm never going to walk away from Travis, no matter how difficult things might be?"

"Yes, I did," Maya admitted, not looking the least bit guilty about it. "But only because I think we both needed to see exactly what your instincts, and your heart, are telling you."

But Amy had already known, hadn't she? Just as Maya had said only moments before, when you love someone, that means whenever that person needs you, you will be there for them. No matter what.

"I can't force him to change his mind," Amy said slowly. "He's got to change it for himself."

"But that's part of the reason you love him, isn't it?" Maya asked. "Because he stands by his beliefs and isn't a man who will turn away from them when the wind blows in the other direction."

"Why did I have to fall in love with someone so strong...and so stubborn?"

"Probably because you know a thing or two about those qualities yourself."

"I'll happily take strong," Amy said. "But stubborn?"

Maya nodded. "Stubborn enough to keep at your art even when your family didn't support you. Stubborn enough to stay friends with me even though I'm on too many planes, too much of the time."

"And stubborn enough to hold fast to my love for Travis," Amy agreed, "no matter how long or winding the road to his heart is."

Maya wrapped her long arms around Amy and hugged her tight. "Now there's the stubborn, strong, amazing woman I know and love."

Amy felt tears come again, but this time they were

tears of appreciation that she had such a good friend in her life. "Nolan really is a lucky guy to have you, you know."

"I tell him that all the time," Maya said with an impish grin. And then, "Do you feel any better? Or did I just make everything worse?"

"I do feel better, actually." Amy took a deep breath to let the ocean air fill her lungs. "I'm not going to lie and say that everything is rainbows and butterflies, when we both know that isn't true. But for the first time in a very long time, at least I know my mind, and my heart. And I have faith that Travis will eventually know his too."

Hopefully sooner rather than later…

# Chapter Twelve

Maya and Nolan's wedding day dawned clear and beautiful.

Married in Malibu had been transformed into an elegant party scene, awash with blues and creams that mirrored the ocean and beach. Their families had already arrived, and a quartet was playing lively Irish reels to celebrate the heritage that Maya and Nolan shared. Actors, models, and musicians who were friends with Maya mingled with Nolan's accountant, engineer, and academic friends. In another setting, the mix might not have worked, but Liz was brilliant at setting the stage for diverse guests to feel comfortable getting to know one another.

And, of course, there were plenty of photographers waiting outside the gates, hoping to catch a glimpse of the supermodel, who was in the bridal suite with her bridesmaids.

Everything was set for another perfect Married in Malibu wedding…and yet Travis wasn't at all sure he'd make it through in one piece.

He hadn't heard from Amy since yesterday afternoon, and hadn't let himself text or call or visit her either. She'd promised to wait for him to change his mind, but he knew that the only way she'd ever be free to find the kind of man she deserved—one without dark stains on his soul—was to make a clean break and go cold turkey.

Somehow, he needed to manage the extra security staff brought in for the day, deal with the endless parade of paparazzi determined to get their shot no matter what, and reassure the famous, wealthy guests that they could let their guards down for once—all while making sure that he didn't run into Amy. So when one of the photographers tried climbing the wall for a better view, Travis almost felt grateful to the guy for providing some distraction.

"Travis!" He was surprised to find Maya hurrying toward him after he made his way back from having a stern word with the photographer. "I need to talk to you."

"Is everything okay?" The last thing anyone wanted at Married in Malibu was an unhappy bride on her wedding day.

"Of course everything isn't okay!"

"Tell me what we can do to help," Travis said.

"You can stop breaking Amy's heart, for starters."

A bolt of pain slashed into his chest at the knowledge that Amy was hurting. Which was why it took several beats longer than it should have for him to remember that he was head of security and couldn't stop doing his job just because his personal life was falling apart.

Knowing the paparazzi would give their left arm *and* their left leg for a photograph of Maya in her wedding dress, Travis quickly took steps to block her from view.

Telling himself he was only doing his job, instead of talking with Maya about Amy, he said, "You shouldn't be out here right now."

"It's my wedding. I can go where I like."

"There are photographers everywhere. It's my job to make sure they don't get shots to sell to the highest bidder."

"Do you think I care about that? You and I need to have a very serious talk, Travis. If we have to do it in full view of photographers, so be it."

Realizing Maya's iron will—and her desire to take care of her best friend—meant that he had no choice but to give in, he said, "Okay, we can talk. But can we *please* do it inside?"

Nodding, she followed him into his office. Once they were inside, she said, "Do you know why I decided to have my wedding at Married in Malibu when I could have gone to the Rose Chalet in San Francisco, or even arranged it in Paris?" She pinned him with a laser-sharp look. "Because I knew you work here."

He was stunned. "You *deliberately* booked your wedding here because you wanted Amy to see me again?" If anything, he would have thought the exact opposite—that Maya would have been desperate to shield her friend from a guy who had proved himself to be heartless.

"I would do anything for Amy. And if you truly loved her, so would you."

"I *would* do anything for her," Travis insisted.

"Anything except accept her love in the same open and honest way that she loves you." Maya didn't pull a single punch. "Anything except actually doing the work to get over your past, no matter how difficult, so that you can be with her."

"I'm sorry," he said in his politest voice, even as the words came from between clenched teeth. "But I really don't think my life is your business."

"You'd better believe it is when it's my best friend you're hurting by not coming to your senses. I asked Amy to come here early this week to make absolutely sure that the two of you would have to spend time together. And for a little while there, it looked like you might finally have gotten things right. But then you went and blew it." She was pacing his office in her gown, getting more riled up by the moment. "I tried setting her up with plenty of great guys over the years. Men with looks, success, money—who were also kind and generous."

Though he didn't have a right to be jealous, Travis couldn't fight back the surge of possessiveness at hearing about these other men.

"But nothing I did to make Amy happy worked," Maya declared. "Because she *couldn't* be happy. Not when she was still desperately, totally in love with you. Being 2,500 miles away in Michigan and having three years pass since the last time you saw or spoke to one another didn't change how she feels about you."

Sitting hard on the edge of his desk, he asked, "Why are you telling me this?"

"Because you need to see just how badly you've blown everything by walking out on her. Again!" Maya gestured to his office and then out the window at her wedding guests. "Is this really enough for you? Is this really all you want out of life? To protect famous brides and grooms from photographers?"

"I'm keeping people safe."

"You're keeping *yourself* safe," Maya snapped back. "Safe from ever having to take a risk with your heart. Safe from ever having to put yourself in someone else's hands."

Travis started to rise to that, then stopped himself. He'd had a lifetime to practice being calm, to work on not giving in to his negative emotions. Especially when someone was poking him exactly where it hurt the most.

A knock came at the door before he could respond. Not that he had known what to say when he felt more broken now by the hard truths Maya had spoken than he ever had by his father's and brother's fists.

Recognizing Meg's and Kate's voices in the hallway, he opened the door to find them both looking extremely anxious.

"Meg, Kate, what is it?" If there was a security problem, it was his job to deal with it, no matter how torn apart he was on the inside.

"Sorry to interrupt your conversation, Maya, but we need Travis to come take a look at something."

"Is anything wrong?" Maya asked.

"Nothing we won't be able to deal with," Kate assured her. "In fact, why don't I take you back to your dressing room? I know Amy and your other bridesmaids are wondering where you are."

Maya nodded, but before she left the office, she gave Travis a look that made it clear she had expected better from him.

She wasn't the only one.

"I hope that was nothing serious?" Meg said.

Unable to answer her question honestly, Travis didn't even try. "What did you come to talk to me about?"

"We have a problem. A big one. Amy has agreed to

try to keep Maya in the dressing room for as long as she can, but we don't have that much time to sort things out."

"Have photographers gotten somewhere they shouldn't?"

"I wish it was something that simple." She took a breath, then hit him with it. "The groom is missing."

# Chapter Thirteen

Liz and Nate were waiting in Nate's office, squeezed in between the computers, monitors, servers, and seemingly endless coils of wires. Jenn, Daniel, and Kate would remain in the hall and gardens to keep the festivities running smoothly until they could find Nolan.

"Meg told me the broad strokes of what happened," Travis said to Liz. "Do we have any idea where Nolan went? And should we alert Maya to the situation?"

"Unfortunately," Liz replied, "he didn't leave any clues. But we've discussed things with Amy, and she agrees that it's better if Maya doesn't know just yet."

"No bride wants to hear that her groom has run off just minutes before she walks down the aisle," Nate commented in a wry voice. "It kind of ruins the mood."

"Travis," Liz said, "you've spent more time talking with him that any of us. Did he say anything that might give you an idea of why he might have gone? Or where?"

It wasn't much of a stretch to look back on the conversation he'd had with Nolan in the gardens, where Travis had been saying he could never be good enough for Amy. Though he'd tried to smooth things over at the end, the truth was that he'd been too wrapped up in his own emotions to set Nolan back to rights. Instead of helping convince Nolan that everything was okay, he'd clearly exacerbated the other man's fears.

"It's my fault." He needed to own up to what he'd done, even if he didn't feel right divulging the actual details of their conversation.

"I don't see how the groom doing a runner could possibly be your fault," Liz said.

Knowing they didn't have time to argue about it right now, Travis simply said, "Trust me, it is. But I'm going to fix it by finding him and convincing him that marrying Maya today will be the best decision he ever makes."

"Okay, but no search parties. Amy is the only one not on staff who knows about this, at least for now. And I'd like to keep it that way if we can."

"She's practically one of us anyway," Nate said. He looked around. "What? She might not have accepted the job yet, but she's going to. I mean, who would turn a gig here down, especially when you can do what you love?"

Travis knew it wasn't as simple as that—love never was, it seemed—but right now he had a groom to find. Especially given that it had been his focus on his own love life, rather than Nolan's, that had helped get them into this mess. It was up to him to get them out of it.

"Nate, can you pull up the security feeds?" A few taps on the keyboard brought them up. "Let's rewind to the last point where we can see Nolan still mingling with the guests."

One of Travis's best skills was the ability to pick faces out of a crowd. It was vital for catching journalists trying to push through a gate in the middle of a group, or spotting a photographer following a client, or picking out a crazy fan in disguise. Travis had never thought, however, that he would use the skill to find a missing groom.

"There," he said, pointing at one of the screens. "I see him. Now move slowly across the feeds from the nearby cameras so that we can see which way he went." At Travis's direction, Nate panned from one camera to the next. "Now over to the garden doors." At last, Travis knew exactly where he was. "He headed towards the beach."

Nolan had been particularly interested in the private cove when they'd been checking out the security setup the day before. Right now, the cameras confirmed that Maya's fiancé had just climbed up on the rocky promontory that separated Married in Malibu's private cove from the wider beach around it.

"He's not going to do anything stupid, is he?" Meg

asked.

"I hope not," Travis replied. "I'm guessing he was just looking for somewhere to think things through. I'll be back with him soon," Travis promised.

Everyone looked at him skeptically, and he understood why. Normally, he wasn't the kind of guy to talk about his feelings. Not when he'd spent most of his life making sure that people never got past his careful boundaries, guarding them as carefully as he now guarded the boundary fences at Married in Malibu.

Even so, it had to be him.

"I can do this," he assured them. "For a start, it's my job to keep everyone here safe, which means I can't let any of you start clambering up steep and unsteady rocks. Plus, though I believe I helped cause this situation to occur, at the same time, I think I understand where he's coming from. So I know how to help him."

Liz stared at him for a long moment before finally nodding. "Okay, then go bring him back. The last thing we want is for the world to hear that Married in Malibu is where grooms disappear from their weddings and then fall off cliffs."

On his way out of Liz's office, Travis was surprised to find Amy coming toward him. "I thought you were supposed to be with Maya," he said.

"I've left a couple of the bridesmaids with her. I needed to check on what's happening. There's only so long I'm going to be able to keep her from figuring out that something's wrong. And I really don't like keeping things from the people I care about."

If she was trying to tell him how much it had hurt that he hadn't talked to her about his past, Travis already knew that. And he wished more than anything that he could beg her for forgiveness, but he had a wedding to save.

"We've figured out where Nolan is," Travis told her, even though there were a million other things he wanted to say. *I love you so much, even if I haven't been acting that way. I'm sorry I keep hurting you. I wish more than anything that I could be good enough for you.* "I'm going to talk with him and convince him to come back."

Even if he could never make things up to Amy or be the man she needed, at the very least he could fix her best friend's wedding.

* * *

Travis scrambled his way up the backside of the rocky outcrop, almost making it to the top before Nolan noticed him. He sat down next to the other man, feeling the sea spray on his skin and the cold hardness of the stone beneath him.

"I thought I'd come out to see if I could help with anything."

Nolan was clearly wrecked. Miles worse than he'd

seemed in the garden the day before. "I blew it."

"You haven't blown it. Not yet. Not if we can get you back to the wedding before Maya knows you've gone."

But Nolan shook his head. "I was standing out there with our wedding guests, and I got to the point where I couldn't take it anymore, not when I could tell what all of them are thinking. That there's no way I should be with her. That she deserves someone a million times better." There was a desperate edge to his voice. "One day she'll thank me for not marrying her. Once I'm out of the picture, she'll find someone as perfect as her, and they'll have a perfect life together."

It was the same thing Travis had told himself over and over about Amy, but hearing it from Nolan—and knowing how devastated Maya would be over losing the man she loved—made the reasons suddenly sound hollow.

"Are you sure you really believe leaving Maya at the altar is the right thing to do? Because I've seen the way you look when you're together. I see how much you love her. We all do."

Nolan picked up a pebble and lobbed it toward the waves. It bounced twice, then sank. "It's not just about what I feel. It's about doing what's right for her. If I love her, then that also means I want her to be the happiest she can possibly be, right? Whatever that costs me."

Travis looked back toward the wedding party, thinking about how Maya glowed whenever Nolan was near. "She seems really happy to me, Nolan."

"But she could have picked anyone she wanted. She could have had a billionaire, or an actor, or a director, or—"

"You're right," Travis interrupted. "Maya could have any guy she chose. But she chose *you*. You've said how much you love her. But have you stopped to think about how much she loves you too?"

That seemed to catch Nolan off guard. "I…"

"You've been so worried about whether you can be what Maya needs that you haven't thought about what *she* truly wants. And what she wants, more than anything else in the word, is to marry *you*."

Nolan swallowed. "I hadn't thought about it like that."

"When you're in a room together, when you look at her, it's like the rest of the world doesn't exist, isn't it? Do you think there's anyone else out there who will ever look at Maya the way you do? That will see the *real* her and love her as much as you do?"

Looking into the mirror of another man's life and seeing the huge mistake Nolan was about to make helped Travis finally see things clearly: No one would ever love Amy the way he loved her. Because he didn't want to change one single thing about her. Caring, stubborn, talented. He loved every side, ever contour, every shade and shadow of her.

It was, he suddenly realized, exactly what she had been trying to tell him. That the darkness in his past didn't turn her away, because she not only accepted every part of him, she also loved him for exactly who his past had helped him become.

Though Travis couldn't force Nolan to return to his wedding, he could give him the truth—one that Travis had run from himself for way too long.

"I've spent a long time in your shoes," Travis said. "Feeling like I'm not worthy. Feeling like I don't have enough to give. Coming up with dozens of reasons why leaving the woman I love is the right thing to do. When it turns out the truth is that loving someone—truly loving them with everything inside of you—means getting over your own fears so that you can give them every piece of your heart. Even when it's hard, even when it's scary. Especially then."

Looking over at Nolan, Travis was extremely happy to note the change in the other man's expression as he said, "You know what? You're right. It's time to get the hell over myself, isn't it?" Nolan ran a rough hand through his hair. "If you hadn't come out here just now, I would have blown absolutely everything."

"In that case, what do you say we climb off this rock, dry you off a bit, and get you your happy ever after?"

Several minutes later, they arrived at the door, where Liz was waiting for them, wearing a very relieved smile.

Travis wanted nothing more than to find Amy and apologize for being a total fool.

He wanted to make sure she knew how he truly felt about her—that he loved her so much, he was finally ready to face his deepest fears, because she was more important than anything else.

He wanted her to know that, if she would still have him after all the ways he'd screwed up, he would officially be the luckiest man on the planet.

But when the first bars of *The Wedding March* sounded, Amy had her duties as maid of honor to attend to, while he had to keep on top of every aspect of security. Even though every minute apart from her—and every second of wondering if she would even consider taking him back—was going to be absolute torture.

*Chapter Fourteen*

Amy was so grateful when Liz whispered that Nolan was on his way back that she would have jumped for joy if that wouldn't have tipped off Maya. Instead, she concentrated on putting the final touches to her friend's outfit, hair, and makeup before stepping back to take one last look.

Anne Farleigh, the dress designer from Married in Malibu's partner company, the Rose Chalet, had created an absolutely incredible white silk-and-lace wedding gown for Maya. What's more, her makeup and hair could have been shot for a commercial.

Yet, none of that even mattered. All that mattered was Maya's radiant glow of happiness.

"How do I look?" Maya sounded nervous about it, which would have seemed impossible to anyone but Amy.

"You're the most beautiful bride I've ever seen." Amy clasped her friend's hands in hers. "How do you feel?"

Maya's heart was in her eyes. "Head over heels in love with Nolan. I can't wait another second for our forever to officially begin."

"I know Nolan feels exactly the same way about you," Amy said, her throat tight with the tears she was willing away so that she didn't set Maya off and ruin the bride's makeup right before saying *I do*. "Now, let's get you down that aisle."

★ ★ ★

As Travis watched Maya enter on her father's arm—a look of pure love on Nolan's face as he watched the woman he adored come down the aisle toward him—there was no arguing with the fact that she was a very beautiful bride. But as far as Travis was concerned, she didn't hold a candle to Amy, who was holding the train of Maya's wedding dress.

And as he watched Maya take her place beside No-lan, Travis hoped with everything in him that one day, he would be the one waiting there for Amy. Ready to give her his heart.

Forever.

★ ★ ★

"When I was a little girl," Maya said, looking deeply into Nolan's eyes as she clasped his hands to her heart, "whenever I would read fairy tales, I would dream that I was the star of the story." Everyone laughed, especially the photographers and photo editors who knew just what a ham Maya could be. "But then we met, and I realized that no fairy-tale hero could ever be as wonderful as you. There's nothing more beautiful to me than the sound of your laughter, the touch of your hand, the love in your eyes. I love you, Nolan, and I can't wait to spend the rest of my life with you."

Amy was glad she had made sure to wear waterproof mascara today, because there was no way that she could listen to Maya speak her vows for Nolan without crying.

Just as there was no way for Amy to keep from imagining one day saying her own vows to Travis.

★ ★ ★

"From the very first day we met," Nolan said to Maya, "I couldn't believe how lucky I was. Not only because you agreed to go out with me, but because you even noticed me in the first place."

Travis moved closer, edging around the guests. Partly to make sure he was in the best position to protect the bride and groom—but mostly because he wanted the best possible vantage point from which to hear Nolan's vows.

"I could hardly believe that we fit together so perfectly, when you're so incredible, and I'm just a lawyer from Michigan. I kept trying to make sense of the equation, but I couldn't."

Everyone in the crowd was holding their breath by now, including Travis. Everyone except Maya. Where another bride might have been panicking by now, her faith in the love she shared with Nolan didn't seem to be wavering even the slightest bit.

Just as Amy refused to waver when it came to Travis.

No doubt about it, Travis and Nolan truly *were* the luckiest guys on the planet. And it was up to them to do whatever necessary to prove that faith was warranted.

"But then," Nolan continued, "I realized the only thing that needs to make sense is that we *are* perfect for one another, no matter how unlikely it might seem. I might be just an ordinary guy, but when I'm with you, I feel extraordinary. I can't imagine what my life would be like without you, Maya, and I don't ever want to. From this moment forward, I promise that I will always be there for you, that I will love you and protect you, and that I will move heaven and earth to try to be everything you need me to be."

★ ★ ★

As Liz declared Maya and Nolan husband and wife, Amy shed another bucketful of tears. Not only because she was absolutely thrilled for her friends and their happiness, but because she couldn't help wondering just how big of a hand Travis had had in helping Nolan see the light.

And if he had helped Nolan see that he was worthy of Maya, then did that mean Travis now felt that *he* could be worthy of love for himself too?

Amy was desperate to run across the room, take Travis's hand, and find a private spot where they could talk. But not only did he have his job to focus on, as maid of honor she also had a vital role to play in gathering everyone for pictures, helping Maya remove a few of the more elaborate accessories from her gown so that she could sit comfortably to eat, giving her speech…and trying not to pass out from nerves when her painting was unveiled.

★ ★ ★

By the time Maya and Nolan started cutting their cake an hour later, Amy was really, really nervous. They would be moving on to the gifts next, opening only a few in front of the guests. But she knew there was no way they would save hers for later. Not when the velvet covering practically begged to be pulled off.

Her heart raced as Maya and Nolan finally made their way to the piles of gifts. They unwrapped a couple of boxes before reaching for the velvet covering.

Amy was almost on the verge of hyperventilating when she felt someone's fingers touch hers. Travis was standing beside her, and his presence alone calmed her as Maya and Nolan finally removed the velvet.

Maya gasped. "Amy, it's wonderful! I can't believe you painted this for us as a surprise."

"It really is great," Nolan agreed.

As all the guests gathered around Amy and her painting, wanting to get a closer look, with one final stroke of his fingers against her palm, Travis disappeared back into the crowd.

\* \* \*

Making sure he was present for Amy's big moment had been like playing a massive game of chess among the tightly packed wedding guests. But it had been more than worth it to ensure the other security guards were in place so that he could be there when Maya and Nolan saw Amy's painting for the first time.

She deserved every bit of praise heaped on her. Her parents and siblings had never appreciated her gift, but he planned to appreciate every last thing about her every single day for the rest of their lives.

He wished he could pull her into his arms in front of everyone and kiss her, but his earpiece had sounded with new security issues to attend to.

With one last glance at her glowing face, he forced himself to go do his job. He hoped he'd be able to steal a few moments from the wedding soon to let Amy know how proud he was of her.

And that he loved her more than he'd even known it was possible to love.

★ ★ ★

The speeches were beautiful, as Maya and Nolan's close friends praised their love and devotion to each other. Amy's speech came last, and her heart felt ready to burst by the time she finally stood and took the microphone.

"The day Maya and I met three years ago was far from my best. I had recently moved to Michigan and was heartbroken, scared, and feeling more than a tad sorry for myself. But nothing I did, nothing I said scared her away. From that day forward, she was the best, most steadfast friend I could have ever asked for." She turned to face the glowing bride. "Maya, you taught me how to be strong. You taught me how to be stubborn. And most of all, you taught me how to love. With everything I am, even when it's hard. Even when it's scary. And even," she added with a small smile, "when I'd rather sit in the woods and feel sorry for myself. I'll never be able to repay you—although I have to take a little credit for introducing you to Nolan at that picnic." Everyone was laughing as she raised her glass. "Please join me in toasting Maya and Nolan. May your future be bright and your love endless."

Tears were streaming down Maya's face as she came

to hug Amy. "You're the best friend in the world."

"No, you are," Amy said.

Because if it hadn't been for Maya choosing to have her wedding at Married in Malibu, she would have missed out on rekindling her love with Travis. Maya had risked the happiest day of her life to give Amy another chance at true love. She couldn't ask for a better friend.

After giving them both a few moments to quickly fix their makeup, Liz directed them to get ready for the bouquet toss. Of course Maya winked at Amy, then sent the flowers flying with precision aim, straight into her hands.

\* \* \*

The guests were all finally gone, but unfortunately, Travis wasn't yet done with his duties. He still had to debrief the security staff hired for the day, check news sources to make sure there hadn't been any leaks, then help the rest of the staff with putting chairs on tables and sweeping up litter.

A text buzzed through to his phone, and his heart jumped when he saw it came from Amy's number.

*Meet me? You know where.*

At every other wedding, he'd been the last one out, triple-checking that his list was complete and that everything was locked tight behind him. Tonight, Jenn,

Kate, Daniel, and Nate would have to close up shop without him.

Travis had already waited three years for his happy ever after.

He wasn't going to wait another second longer.

★ ★ ★

Amy stood on the beach in the same spot where she had told Travis she loved him for the very first time, her heart pounding with anticipation.

She didn't have one single doubt that he would come. Just as she didn't have any doubts about how much she loved him—and that they would find a way to make their love work this time around. No matter what.

Which was why she'd sent two additional texts while she was there on the beach.

The first had been to Liz, accepting her job offer.

The second had been to Johan, to let him know that she would bring by several brand-new paintings for him to look at in the next two weeks. Given that she had left all of her work behind in Michigan, she was going to be doing a lot of painting in the very near future.

"Waiting for someone?" Travis asked from behind her.

She spun to throw herself into his arms, her favorite place to be. "You got here so quickly."

"I don't know if I'd call three years quick." He cradled her face in his hands. "I let you down when I walked away because I didn't think I was good enough for you. I didn't think I *could* be good enough for you. But just like Nolan said in his vows to Maya, it doesn't matter if I don't think I'm perfect. The only thing that matters is that I think *you're* perfect—and I have since the first time I set eyes on you. I've loved you from that very first moment, Amy, and I'm not ever going to stop."

"And you're everything I could ever have hoped for in a man," she said in a voice that trembled with emotion.

"Even with the things I've done in the past?"

"I'm so sorry for what you went through," she said softly. "I wish you had been raised by a loving father and that your relationship with your brother had been better too. But you not only rose above your difficult upbringing, you turned it around so that your every thought, every motive, every single act is based in kindness and caring. Never, for one second, doubt how grateful I am that we got a second chance to love each other."

"A third chance," he pointed out in a low voice that resonated with regret for making love to her and then turning her away again over the past twenty-four hours. "We might not ever be able to erase the pain of our pasts, but I'm not going to let that stop us from building a beautiful future together. I never should have walked away from you. If you'll let me make it up to you, I promise I'll never make that mistake again."

"Everything you ever did, you did because you loved me. You left because you thought that it would keep me safe, even though you were wrong about that. All you wanted was what is best for me—when all along *you* have been what's best for me. I want to spend the rest of my life with you. I want to wake up every morning in your arms and fall asleep to the sound of your heartbeat. And as often as we can, I want to come right here to this beach and kiss you. Just like this."

And when they kissed to seal the vows they'd just made to each other on the beach, it wasn't just a kiss worth waiting three years for—it was the kiss of a *lifetime*.

*Epilogue*

Meg had never seen Travis so happy. And Meg was happy, as well, that Amy had accepted Liz's offer to be Married in Malibu's in-house portrait painter. It would be great to have another visually creative person at work to bounce ideas off of.

In any case, it was much more fun to focus on Travis and Amy's happiness than it was to prepare herself to see her mother.

Her childhood home was huge and white-walled, far too large for one woman and her staff. Meg had never felt comfortable there.

Not that she'd been *Meg* while growing up, of course. Her mother wouldn't dream of calling her anything but Margaret. Her mother had focused all her efforts on grooming her only child to be the perfect daughter.

But it hadn't worked. Meg was too quiet. Too serious. She didn't like small talk and wasn't interested in clothes and jewelry either. The only part of that life Meg had enjoyed was putting on events. She had loved transforming shapes and colors and light into something beautiful for everyone to enjoy.

Bertrand, the butler, opened the door, and Meg went through to find that tea was already set out for them. Her mother sat perfectly poised, as though she was posing for one of Amy's paintings.

"Margaret, there you are," her mother said.

Feeling as though she was already treading on egg-shells, Meg sat down. "Hello, Mother."

She hadn't come to visit since she'd started at Married in Malibu and her mother had made her feelings about Meg working for a living, rather than hunting for a wealthy, high-profile husband, clear.

"Have you seen this?" Her mother held up a news-paper clipping of Lucas Crosby, the world-famous singer. "Is it true that this man will be using your married-in-whatever place soon?"

Meg would have had to be blind not to notice that Lucas had a finely chiseled jawline with just the right amount of stubble, sandy hair down to his shoulders, and piercing blue eyes. Butterflies swam in her stomach at the thought of meeting him.

"Yes, as far as I know, he will be coming to shoot a video with us."

Her mother threw the paper down, obviously dis-gusted. "If only we didn't have to read about people like this all the time. I really don't know how you manage to deal with all those horrible models and actors and singers, walking around as if they've got *real* money."

By which she meant *old money*, of course. On any other day, Meg might have left it. She might not have answered back. Indeed, she'd spent her life very carefully not talking back to her mother, because she had hoped that one day, her mother might show her the same love and respect that Meg had always shown to her.

Now, though, Meg couldn't allow her mother to assume the worst about the people Married in Malibu worked for.

"They're all actually quite lovely."

"Lovely?" Her mother sounded like she'd just swallowed a wasp. "You think that these people, these celebrities, are *lovely*?"

"I do, yes," Meg said. "They're mostly just like you and me."

"They are *nothing* like us," her mother insisted, but then, there were members of royalty who wouldn't be "good enough" either. "This job has rubbed off on you far too much if you're starting to think like that."

If it had, Meg thought, she was glad.

"I should have never allowed you to take the position," her mother continued. "I should have insisted that you refuse it."

"You *did* insist that I not do it," Meg pointed out.

"You insisted quite strongly."

"And yet, even knowing how much it upsets me, you still went ahead with it. Well, it's long past time you returned to your senses and came back to your real life."

Every other time in the last twenty-seven years that Meg's mother had used that tone, Meg had caved. Meg hated arguments, with her mother especially. But she hadn't backed down the day she took the job, and she wasn't going to back down now.

"I'm going to continue working at Married in Malibu," she said, her spine as straight as her mother's and her chin as high, "because I love what I do." She pointed to the picture of Lucas Crosby, taken during a particularly energetic and passionate part of one of his shows. "Look at him, Mother. He loves what he does. Can't you see that? I feel the same way about my career."

Her mother huffed. "No daughter of mine will ever be in the same category as a man like *that*. Good grief, he probably does *drugs*, Margaret. Is that the kind of person you hang around with in this job of yours?"

Meg bit back an angry retort. It was always better, when it came to her mother, to simply leave things and hope that she forgot about them. Which was precisely what Meg had done with her job.

But it hadn't worked, had it? Because she'd made Meg come today not because she missed her and wanted to catch up, but so she could pressure her into quitting.

"Thank you for inviting me to tea." She forced herself to lean in to kiss her mother's cheek. "But I think it might be best if I came again another time. I have a lot to take care of in my office."

"Yes," her mother agreed. "It would be best if you came back when you're ready to see some sense. Here." She shoved the newspaper at Meg. "Take this and throw it away. I can't stand to look at it."

As Meg walked out of the house, she looked at the photo of Lucas Crosby again. He looked so free, leaping toward the cameraman with a huge smile. Meg couldn't imagine what it would be like to be that free, something she'd always longed for.

But even more than freedom, Meg longed for love.

Was there any chance that one day the magic surrounding everyone at Married in Malibu—first Liz and Jason, then Jenn and Daniel, and now Travis and Amy—would rub off on her?

★ ★ ★ ★ ★

**For news on upcoming books, sign up for Lucy Kevin's New Release Newsletter: LucyKevin.com/Newsletter**

# ABOUT THE AUTHOR

Lucy Kevin is the pen name for Bella Andre. Having sold more than 7 million books, Bella Andre's novels have been #1 bestsellers around the world and have appeared on the *New York Times* and *USA Today* bestseller lists 83 times. She has been the #1 Ranked Author on a top 10 list that included Nora Roberts, JK Rowling, James Patterson and Steven King, and Publishers Weekly named Oak Press (the publishing company she created to publish her own books) the Fastest-Growing Independent Publisher in the US. After signing a groundbreaking 7-figure print-only deal with Harlequin MIRA, Bella's "The Sullivans" series has been released in paperback in the US, Canada, and Australia.

Known for "sensual, empowered stories enveloped in heady romance" (Publishers Weekly), her books have been Cosmopolitan Magazine "Red Hot Reads" twice and have been translated into ten languages. Winner of the Award of Excellence, The Washington Post called her "One of the top writers in America" and she has been featured by Entertainment Weekly, NPR, USA Today, Forbes, The Wall Street Journal, and TIME Magazine. A graduate of Stanford University, she has given keynote speeches at publishing conferences from Copenhagen to Berlin to San Francisco, including a standing-room-only keynote at Book Expo America in

New York City.

If not behind her computer, you can find her reading her favorite authors, hiking, swimming or laughing. Married with two children, Bella splits her time between the Northern California wine country, a 100 year old log cabin in the Adirondacks, and a flat in London overlooking the Thames.

For a complete listing of books, as well as excerpts and contests, and to connect with Bella:

**Sign up for Lucy's newsletter:**
**lucykevin.com/newsletter**

**Visit Lucy's website at:**
**www.LucyKevin.com**

**Sign up for Bella's newsletter:**
**BellaAndre.com/Newsletter**

**Visit Bella's website at:**
**www.BellaAndre.com**

**Follow Bella on Twitter at:**
**twitter.com/bellaandre**

**Join Bella on Facebook at:**
**facebook.com/bellaandrefans**

**Follow Bella on Instagram:**
**instagram.com/bellaandrebooks**

Made in the USA
Coppell, TX
09 May 2021